Hollow Water

Hollow Water

stories and
travels by

Pete Sarsfield

TURNSTONE PRESS

Turnstone Press
607 – 100 Arthur Street
Artspace Building
Winnipeg, Manitoba
Canada R3B 1H3
www.TurnstonePress.com

Turnstone Press gratefully acknowledges the assistance of the
Canada Council for the Arts, the Manitoba Arts Council and
the Government of Canada through the Book Publishing Industry
Development Program for our publishing activities.

The Canada Council | Le Conseil des Arts
for the Arts | du Canada

Canadä

Original cover photograph by Greg Di Cresce
Author photo by Morgan Boyd, *Kenora Enterprise*
Cover design: Manuela Dias
Interior design: Marijke Friesen
Printed in Canada by Friesens
for Turnstone Press

Canadian Cataloguing in Publication Data
Sarsfield, Pete, 1944–
Hollow water: stories and travels
ISBN 0-88801-244-6
1. Sarsfield, Peter, 1944–   —Journeys.   I. Title.
R464.S37 A3 2000   C818'.5409   C00-920103-3

for Jan   for Sarah

Contents

Travels

Hollow Water 5
May Month, Hopedale 9
Harmony Within 13
Sandspit Point 17
North/South 19
No Money 23
Avoiding a Common Victory 27
Impolite Company 33

Stories

The Devil You Know 41
Three to Dance 49
Wind Toys, Again 55
Private Joke 59
Jailbirds 63

Travels

Don Quixote at the Holiday Inn 73
I'm Not Leaving Here Forever 83
Greyhound Fashion Consultant 87
Adjudicating Fragments 97
Maugham's Room 101
A Welcome Dread 109
Sheep in Sheeps' Clothing 125

Stories

Flatwater Brook 135
Solving Problems 157
Thick with Rabbits 177
Tide Flats 185

Author's Note

Slightly different versions of a few of these pieces were published previously: "Tide Flats" in the *Pottersfield Portfolio*, "Three to Dance" in the *Dalhousie Review*, and several of the travel pieces in *The Medical Post*.

I've been told that fiction and non-fiction are separable, and different. The fiction of recall and the actuality of imagination have a huge overlap. In spite of this grayness, the ones I've called "stories" are mostly invented, and the "travels" are as close to recalled events as I could get them.

It is enjoyable to thank people: generally, to those friends who behave as family and to those family who behave as friends, and specifically to Benita Cohen, thank you.

—Pete Sarsfield
Kenora, Ontario, 2000

Travels

"I didn't know whether to duck or to run, so I ran"
—Bob Dylan,
in "Brownsville Girl"

Hollow Water

An old map of northern Canada I own and use shows the location of the "Indian Band communities," and on the days when the overriding sensation is one of being too far south, exiled from tundra and solitude, the names give a calming touch. A few I've visited but most not, and yet the names have an evocative capability as they produce nostalgia for places I've not yet seen.

There are the indigenous names, abstract and lyrical to me in my unilingual ethnocentrism, telling me things about the land and people that I am not capable of hearing: *Waywayseecappo*, *Mishkeegogamang*, *Pauingassi*, *Wasagamack*, *Keewaywin*, and *Wapekeka*. Other descriptive place names based on geography and wildlife have a distinctive eloquent terseness that I hope to explore: *Rolling River*, *Muskrat Dam*, *Shoal Lake*, *Long Plain*, and *Big Grassy River*. A few others permit an ironic nod of acknowledgment with their ambiguous twists: *God's Lake Narrows*, *Bloodvein*, *North Spirit Lake*, *Summer Beaver*, and *Gambler*. The most truly sustaining, though, are the ones that manage to give it and take it away all in one motion. My favourites of these are

Ebb and Flow, and *Hollow Water*. What else can we hope for on these dunes, or pretend to achieve, than the ebb and flow of hollow water?

✷ ✷ ✷

Occasionally someone from the north, someone I used to know and run into, will ask what I'm doing now since I've stopped being a northern travelling doc, and I find it difficult to be specific. When I tell the person that I'm an MOH, a Medical Officer of Health, a public health or community medicine doctor, it usually causes eyes to glaze over. "What the hell is *that*?" a valued acquaintance queried, summing up the general response. I shift weight from foot to foot, talking about treating the community instead of the individual and of the need for promotion of health and prevention of illness, trying to find a one-liner that tells what it is I'm doing here. "I'm trying to help people be careful," I recently offered and then had the sense to blush when the person who had asked raised her eyebrows.

A fellow MOH had someone say to her, with disdain, "What? You're going to be a *bureaucrat*?" The ultimate staged dive, actually to work *for* the government instead of throwing rocks *at* it in the true patriotic manner of the thoughtful citizen. My problem, one of my problems, is that, after 25 years of working for governments and other assorted self-serving dinosaurs, I often agree with my colleague's rude critic. Another problem is that most of the Community Medicine training *does* seem to be aiming toward administrative or bureaucratic roles, with precious little emphasis on the community-based issues and dilemmas that I'd been blindly swimming in for the years I was a GP. These are the concerns that led me here in the first place, so my expertise would not always be of the suspect self-taught variety. There seems to be very little community in Community Medicine, however, and a person has to be very tough and very certain of personal signposts, it seems, to do it differently. It *can* be done, though. One of the toughest, and finest, people I know has provided an impressive role model. She first used her public health training to be a travelling doc in northern Labrador, then worked with Health Auxiliaries in Uganda and Ethiopia and Kenya, and is now an MOH in northern BC. In one letter from Africa, she said that there are few sights to equal the darkening of the sky at midday by migrating clouds of bats, an image that brightened my day considerably.

✳ ✳ ✳

It seems that identity confusions of this kind do not end with an insightful and definitive flash, at least not for most of us. On a TV news program a few years ago, an MD in a relatively small Canadian town was interviewed, a surgeon who had carried a huge load for a long time and was now saying "enough," leaving the place where he had worked for over 20 years. He was thin and wasted looking, tired in his eyes and voice and in his way of holding himself. In a plain, sad way, which was apparently empty of guilt or appeal but not, I thought, of anger and bitterness, he told of working long hours, day after day, year after year. He was leaning, casually, against something as he spoke. He said that he now heard how doctors today wanted to have a normal life, to not kill themselves, and then paused before he added that he was learning this many years too late. His face and the tone of his time persist in my memory; they haunt me, as does his style of leaning.

On another TV program, more recently, another interviewer spoke of a doctor in one of the worst hit sub-Sahara drought and hunger areas as a "strange" person, leaving it at that. A few brief footages showed a small man in his late thirties or early forties, with thinning hair flying around as he walked and talked with the local people, in the blowing sand. One view showed him reaching out to touch some people, and they didn't seem to mind, or to find him strange. In a very short clip, this doctor spoke with compassion and energy, and also, interestingly enough, with *humour*, of the need to give hunger and death a run for their money, even though you know you're eventually going to lose. Then he smiled, but there was something else in his eyes, a glint, perhaps a challenge, and I assume it was aimed at something larger than the camera.

The two doctors seemed connected, affiliated, and it seems that they would both know what public health is doing and why. They would certainly understand the sense and rhythm of hollow water.

May Month, Hopedale

May month in Hopedale, Labrador, comes up with surprises: the amazing volume of winter dog shit, the "sinky" snow dropping you sprawling up to one thigh, the sneak snowstorm that stops the plane from coming and (again and again) separates the insiders from the outsiders. It also brings moodiness, a minimalist despair, to many of the outsiders who remember May having green grass and warm air and who are very tired of rotting snow and new mud and surfacing sewage.

A friendly acquaintance phones to say she doesn't know why she came here anyway and just because she made a mistake *then*, doesn't mean she has to make one *now*, not at all, so she just quits and leaves. And I almost can't blame her.

But I *do* blame her. It's so shortsighted to leave, because as awful as parts of May can be, it is highlighted by the fact that it ends and June comes, complete with family time away from the villages, fishing, icebergs, coastal boats, whales, berries, and the all-connecting Labrador Sea. A startling, full time of year, if only you know how to pick your spots, the inevitable qualifying rub.

On this particular wet-snow-and-mud May Day I get lucky, partly just by being reminded of the ongoing rich reality of being alive, at a time when I am in need of reminders. I'm given a guided walk around the town, after having been away from Hopedale for years. The sensations, the fingertips, are gummed up by nostalgia and regret and recollections, some foggy and some accurate. I'm in need of a guide.

We look at gravestones—flat slabs dated in the1850s and 1860s, lying in bare patches of dry winter grass near the retreating drifts of melting snow. On reading some of the names and dates, there is the reflex response of shared sadness and dry unrepentant relief. This is the "old grave-yard," and there aren't many stones, while in the next yard, behind a cleaner fence, is the new graveyard. We don't visit it. The flat stones won't be readable much longer, 20 or 30 years, maybe even a hundred if some person really puts heart into it. I hope it's nobody I know.

The Hopedale hills *will* last, though, in spite of rather than because of us. The trees are gone now, used for fire-wood over the last 150 years. The American Base on the hill is in an appropriate state of obscene decay, with roofs caved in and walls used for buildings or fires, and with piles of tin left which will last a few lifetimes, just so we don't get overly smug about the dust-to-dust possibilities. The twin "early warning" black radar rectangles are still there, huge and alone and separate from everything else, unplugged for years—our own silly monument to other countries' fears. It is unlikely that anyone will ever buy a ticket to see them.

We go to the old Moravian Mission buildings with our guide, who struggles with the English words for Inuit places and things and who has a kind laugh. She lived in Okak in 1918, when so many died from the flu. All her family died, "except two aunties." She was seven.

We are shown around the oldest, decaying, three-storey, white-and-green building. The Moravians have been here creating Christian souls and selling their version of civilization since the mid 1700s, and this building is the oldest in Labrador, an unwilling museum. As we walk around the rooms, it is easy to see that this dead, empty thing once had a purpose, but it has now wandered into lean financial times and spiritually unresponsive times. It's a different symbol now, as it slowly falls in on itself.

We pass through the part of the building where the church service is held, the only heated area and the least valuable to me. I dislike churches, and yet I feel comfortable in them, the always-present juxtaposition of equal and opposite truths, which is a stable foundation. Our guide made the vestments, "years ago," and they are beautiful, green with delicate clear embroidery. Several pages have been burned from the pastor's large hymnbooks, probably having been left too close to the stove. The heat from the stove is very fine on this damp May 1st.

In the attic, the minister who left recently had made an effort to organize and save bits of the area's past. The mixture, again, is overwhelming. Boxes of unopened hymnbooks, in German, old medicine bottles in rows with seals intact but all hint of names and purpose gone, personal diaries in English and German, unused school books in English from the 1920s, and the room has a window with most of the glass smashed out.

As we leave, I again feel both loss and relief, walking out of the building into the snow, which is intent on melting us toward summer.

11

Harmony Within

We are five in the medium-sized car, all a bit restless and aware that we have 1400 kilometres ahead of us, and that the rough road demands a leisurely approach. We've set up this crowded marathon drive by choice, but also by necessity. The bureaucratic whim of the week, emitted by the geniuses who are funding our trip to the conference in Alaska, dictated that government money could not be spent flying outside of Canada. O.K., we said, in search of the always-present Plan B, how about if we fly to Whitehorse, Yukon, Canada, and rent a car, a Canadian car, then drive to Anchorage, U.S.A. Deal? Deal. So off we go.

We recognize trees and rivers, burned-over areas with regrowth underway, hills and curves, frost heaves and potholes, and the mountains toy with the middle and edges of our sight. We stop in Haines Junction for a quick slideshow at the tourist place. It's May month and they're just warming up, doing a stretching exercise before the real game with the block-long RVs. The highlight of the stop is the café where the cinnamon rolls are legendary-huge and the waiter has a quick flashing sense of humour that leads us to ask her to join the trip, and we mean it. She declines, but it seems to us that there was a moment of telltale hesitation.

We drive beside the St. Elias range in Kluane National Park, then around Kluane Lake, a long ice-filled mountain-circled beauty that allows us to stop and watch it. Later from the car we see a bear, then several moose and caribou, and mountain goats or sheep as moving white patches on a steep hillside, far up.

As we approach the U.S. border I get anxious, partly due to all those Checkpoint Charlie movies ingested as a kid and partly from having been hassled several times, and arrested once, at similar Canada-U.S.A. borders. The U.S. Customs person has a drawl and a clear gaze; seemingly friendly, he is watching everything. He asks us a few questions just to hear our voices, our accent and tone and ease of response, and to observe our eyes and hands. Then he waves us on; five minutes, no problem.

The drive to Tok, Alaska, is over the worst roads of the day, gravel, construction, and *rough*. We limp into Tok, which has six motels, an as-yet unopened Tourist Bureau, three restaurants, an abandoned laundromat, and even a few houses. We are tolerated at one of the motels, although the owners are not happy with our Canadian credit cards, rumour of their poor cousins' downward-sliding dollar having reached Tok. It appears that this rumour has not been accompanied by notice of the credit card companies' inclination to charge in American funds while we're in the rich U.S. of A. We win the financial debate, but not by much. Six hundred and fifty kilometres under our drive belt today, and we feel like lost foreigners who've blundered into a small hostile western town.

The next day we go through some of the most

spectacularly strange and beautiful mountain and alpine-meadow land any of us has ever seen. In the car, we are a mixture of friends, work colleagues, and strangers; two from Labrador, one from Winnipeg, one from the Northwest Territories, and one from British Columbia. We don't talk much, avoiding home truths this far from home. We watch the land. Mount Noyes is off to our left for over two hours, a huge peak with the covering snow thick, round and smooth, "like an ice cream cone," one usually quiet rider says. It is named after a Brigadier-General, our map and books ignoring the name used by Aboriginal people for thousands of years before we came along. We see more animals and more moving views than we can cope with, so we become overwhelmed and subdued as we drive slowly into Anchorage.

There was a severe earthquake here in the 1960s, and most of the buildings look relatively new, square and low. The city has mountains at its back and sides, a harbour out front with ships on the move, U.S. military planes manoeuvring overhead, many shops with fine and expensive "native crafts," as well as queues of drunks and prostitutes outside the hotel on 4th Avenue.

Only three of us will be driving back, as two decide they've enjoyed as much as they can stand and book flights through Vancouver. The three returnees don't spend much time together during the week in Anchorage, but we do go looking for a quiet restaurant on one of the last evenings. We find one with excellent vegetarian food, warm and gentle solo guitar music, and a large banner on the wall advertising HARMONY WITHIN.

The guitarist came from San Francisco years ago. He is also a potter who owns a large piece of land, or so we're told. We clap for his songs and he nods at us.

Perhaps we'll stop again for a cinnamon roll in Haines Junction on the way back. It *is* a two-way street, after all.

Sandspit Point

I am saying goodbye, for now. As I wander around the Kitikmeot Region of the Arctic I remember a piece I read recently, "The Allure of the Azores" by Douglas Bell, in which he talks briefly about the Portuguese concept of "saudade." This attitude is described as requiring acts of "ritual remembrance," which are a combination of "devotion, longing, and melancholy." Saudade; I do like the sound of that, as I walk again to the steep rock bluff near the river, a few miles south of Pelly Bay, and later the same week at Gjoa Haven visit the curving wide sweep of rocky beach, still sitting frozen in ice. Acts of ritual remembrance; walks to live by.

Outside Spence Bay, now more appropriately named Taloyoak, I go to my favourite walking spot in the Kitikmeot, Sandspit Point. This is a narrow finger of sand poking out into the bay portion of St. Roch Basin. It has two small round ponds near the middle, and waiting for the summer fishing are a tent, an oil-drum stove, and a fish-drying rack, perched in a family cluster at the very end of the mile-long point.

In August and early September, before the bay has frozen and while the evenings are still bright, you can lean against a round-backed boulder and watch the Arctic Ocean nudge at the shore. I am more familiar with the force of the Atlantic, having spent much of my life at the coastal edge of Nova Scotia and Labrador. It seems that the Arctic Ocean lacks the smells, seaweed, fishing boats, sun-tanning beaches, and erratic malevolence of a real ocean. The summer ocean is instead only a subdued three-month partially thawed hiatus for the genuine Arctic Ocean, the real thing, which is the frozen sea of true ice.

This type of geographic chauvinism is much easier to maintain from a safe and solitary rock niche on Sandspit Point, wrapped in a winter parka in August and sheltered from the winds of St. Roch by the bulk of Cape Isabella. I don't know the names in Inuktitut for *any* of these places.

Despite my ignorance, the Point has been good to me, like so much else in the Kitikmeot. My plan is to adopt a modified *saudade* approach to the Kitikmeot, and to Sandspit Point, the Arctic; all of it. I'll emphasize the devotion and ritual remembrance, and play down the melancholy. The other part, the longing, I can respond to; I can come back.

North/South

Mid-September—I arrive at 5:20 pm at the departure counter for the 5:30 pm flight to Rankin Inlet from Winnipeg, to the tight-lipped, eye-rolling exasperation of the ticket agent. It is obvious to me that the more ambivalent I am about a trip, the closer to the wire I cut my check-in, not a particularly subtle form of fate-tempting, passive-aggressive behaviour. (Not an effective one either: I make the flight.)

Marcy is the flight attendant on this four-propeller Electra trip. In the three years during the mid 1980s that I moved around the Kitikmeot Region of the NWT, mostly on DC-3s, Marcy was one of the most skilled and memorable flight attendants. She was usually polite and cheerful, even when shifting freight, missed landings because of ice, fog and wind, and the subsequently grumpy passengers led her to feel otherwise. Her public relations ability was extraordinary; she was a high-intensity charmer, full of inoffensive banter and a genuine urge to help. She would also talk about real things, and we sat through hundreds of hours between Yellowknife, Coppermine, Pelly Bay,

Spence Bay, Gjoa Haven, and Cambridge Bay, talking about any issue that dropped into the tangential flow. Now, several years later, Marcy is working this flight, and we spend most of the three hours exchanging details of where our lives have gone and are going. We have both become a bit more jaded and a lot more cautious. Our stories have a sad edge, but we are making our own choices, more or less. It is a pleasure to share another flight with her.

＊ ＊ ＊

Rankin Inlet has a crowded terminal, with the name in syllabics over the door, and it is fine to hear the throaty cadence of Inuktitut again. Only one of the three community taxis has met the plane, so the person I'm traveling with and I decide to walk the mile to the hotel.

It is 8:30 p.m., the air is sharp, blowing at +5°C, and it's almost dark. There is a half-moon just off the horizon, and I'm interested to see that there's not even a hint of ice at the water's edge. Cambridge Bay's ponds would usually be starting to freeze by now, and the 2½-mile walk to town from that airport in mid-September could be painful, especially with bare hands holding luggage. On this Keewatin evening, however, life is a clear-aired, tolerable breeze, with all-terrain vehicles buzzing at our edges but not intruding, not overwhelming this Central Arctic walk. I'm ashamed of my earlier airport check-in ambivalence and leave it on the road to the hotel, somewhere between the parked grader and the Co-op store, just past the pond and opposite the school.

The meeting that goes on for the next three days symbolizes the changing Arctic, at least in this one corner. It is held in the Siniktarvik hotel, in a plush, sterile, efficient, non-smoking meeting room, complete with muffins and tea and simultaneous translation connected to individual battery-operated receivers. We eat in a well-stocked dining room and sleep in comfortable single rooms with cable TV and an unending supply of hot water in the shower. This is a very long distance from the smoky, crowded, sometimes noisy and sometimes silent but always chaotic meetings I was weaned on, and I have to admit I miss the old way, even the cloud of smoke. This way has a written agenda, which we more or less follow, and we are very aware of protocol and process. If we're lucky, the lack of colour and bounce will be balanced by a productive efficiency. I try not to count on being lucky.

In the evenings after the meeting and mornings before it starts, I go for long walks, to gather images. They come in clusters—the sight and sound of three-wheelers on dirt roads, the feel of tundra and horizon once I'm away from the edge of town, running out from the eye for miles, uninterrupted by trees. Inuit travellers to the south will sometimes complain of the visual interference of trees and of the resulting claustrophobia, much as those who live on the prairie and beside the ocean can't bear the mountains for too long. In the years I lived north of the tree line, I missed trees, very much, but it is good to be out on the tundra again. I'm not home here, but I'm not alien, either.

A ground squirrel lets out a quick startled yelp when I blunder near to its nest, an old rusted length of half-buried sewage pipe so that the animal has front door and back door and several decades worth of round-walled shelter. Perhaps the Arctic can absorb all the garbage we send its way and convert it to use, but I doubt it.

On the second day of the meeting, my presentation

falls flat, with a thud, missing the mood and concerns of the group by a wide mark. Instead of doing what I usually do, which is relate stories to themes, an approach learned from the Innu and Settlers and Inuit of Labrador, I bow to the intimidation of advice and the aura of the neo-fancy hotel, using dry numbers and overhead graphs and a scientific order of "facts." The presentation falls so flat that I'm asked to stop half-way through, with moderate politeness, but a definite hook nevertheless. I am angry with myself for having been so easily faked out by the decor and surface details, and for forgetting the realities of bridging-the-gap communication. It appears that I have to relearn the same lessons, time after time. Failure is always such an achingly wonderful opportunity for personal growth.

✳ ✳ ✳

It feels good to leave when the return plane comes in, good to have been here *and* good to leave. I must be at a crossroads to have that happen but cannot for the life of me see the signs, not on the angled runway, not in the palpable absence of Marcy on this flight, not in my crashing failure of a presentation, none of it. What would poetmaster Frost have done, with that snowy quizzical horse, if the road hadn't been so blatant, so overtly forked? Oh, what the hell, relax and have a good flight, crossroads on the highway-of-angst be damned. I'm going to move in with that ground squirrel and subvert the rest of the century to my very own purpose.

Do ground squirrels have fireplaces? Why not?

No Money

A few of us government-paid health-care types fly into Summer Beaver, Ontario, to answer some questions about a 20,000-gallon gasoline spill that happened over a year ago, and has yet to be cleaned up. In fact, it has yet to receive serious government attention of any kind. Several organizations and departments have debated who's on first, including: three federal government departments, a provincial public health unit and two provincial government departments, a regional Tribal Council and its consultants, two private fuel transport and supply companies, and the community Band Council. Apparently, absolutely no-one is on first as absolutely no-one assumes or accepts the lead. So it goes; we are about to receive a much deserved public spanking.

Summer Beaver is the English language name for Nibinamick First Nation, a community of several hundred Anishinabe (Ojibway, in old English), situated hundreds of kilometres directly north of Thunder Bay. It is surrounded by lake and boreal forest. The woods immediately surrounding the town are mostly standing dead spruce, skinny and barren, as a forest fire flirted with the edges of the town a few years ago. In the natural cycle of things this fire did not hurt the land, and the burned-over forest floor is now rich with berries and shrubs in summer, and the standing dead trees are an easy source of firewood. The new thick growth of brush and poplar and fledgling spruce is underway. In the midst of this, all the buildings in the town are either made of logs, or have log-like siding, and it works. This is a beautiful place.

We get taken to the school gym at 1 pm for the 1 pm meeting, and we're the first ones there; the place is empty, bare. We're early, which is a polite and cross-culturally cautious way of acknowledging that there's *no way* that this or any other "meeting" in Aboriginal country is ever going to start on time. This is only a problem for us outsiders, and it's our fault anyway that we're booked on the 3:30 pm flight "out," this very same day. If we had a brain or even a righteous bone, collectively speaking, we'd have planned for an overnight stay, out of respect if intelligence was out of the question.

Our "early" arrival to the meeting-place school gym gives me a chance to root out a basketball and attempt a few three-pointers at one end of the deserted floor. I'm awful, which is standard, but I continue to feel that I'll eventually achieve the touch, the wrist and finger-tip flip and roll, swish, nothing but net from *far* downtown. It doesn't happen, but a few people do start to drift in, chairs and tables are found, and the meeting gets underway at about 2 pm. There are now more than fifty community residents in the folding-chair seats, and five of us bureau-crats are perched on display at the front, two government-paid, one Tribal Councillor, a Band Council representative, and a translator. Impending spanking or not, I do love these community meetings. They are the closest thing to true public accountability that I see in any aspect of my life. It seems to work, and as with the log buildings, even those with the fake log-siding, it produces cohesiveness.

We get grilled, about finances and accountability and righteousness and intelligence, and we don't come out of it looking very good. The questions and comments directed at us are polite, respectful even, but there's no mistaking the fact that we have been measured and found to be inadequate. We promise to study some budgets and papers, and to do-the-best-we-can in the midst of an inflexible and uncaring world. There *are* days when self-loathing is an entirely apt reflex.

There is one moment that brings me fully alert, and it happens so casually, so gently and without the jugular-seeking, chest-pounding self-congratulation that is so revered in my culture. This moment comes when the Tribal Council person is responding to the government-paid plea of "no available funds." He says (and being without shame to the bitter end, I quickly grab a pen to write it down), "When they say there's no money, they don't mean there's no money. What they mean is, there is no money for *you*." He delivers this quietly, politely, and the only responses from the public seats are a few gentle nods and smiles. I admire the room, their part of the room.

We miss our flight, as is only just. However, just to show what we *do* have money for, a plane is chartered to take us home.

Do we hang our heads? Perhaps we do, every one of us, but we keep it so much to ourselves.

Avoiding a
Common Victory

A person I worked with for a short while several years ago used to say, "I reserve the right to be confused," as a defense and offense against those who were so damned sure of their silly little one-sided truths, like me for instance. I've never had a problem with having definite opinions about things, about any old thing at all, whether I know a speck about the topic or not, since it has always seemed easier to move from dead certainty to flat-out confusion rather than the other way around. There are many like me and we could form a club, holding daily meetings with testimonies that rave on, scorning those of faint opinion.

For some years now, however, I've been having problems with the increasing roaring swarm of what a scholarly ex-friend refers to, with adroit self-mockery, as "cognitive dissonance." I am awash in the apparent clash of truths, and the cogs are grinding, loud and foul. Confusion is in the room.

On this full sunlight morning, 8:00 am, I'm driving as almost-free as a land-bound bird, from Kenora to Winnipeg, to get aboard a plane to Sault Ste. Marie. On the way, near Prawda, Manitoba, I listen to the CBC radio morning commentary.

It's by a "military analyst," telling us why we need, *really* need, to continue the low-level military training flights over Labrador, which started a decade ago. He tells how the end of the cold war has not meant an end to our need for armed strength, for "security," and that our ever-so-skillful flying killers-in-training need to practice so they can deliver their "payloads," should we ever need to settle some particular account in full. He is an ex-Colonel, now working for a company that worries out loud about *our* security, when hired to do so, and he mentions that Labrador is ideal for this preparation for war. We're told that the pilots take pride in not inconveniencing any "settlements" or wildlife, and should the occasional minor annoyance occur, it's a small and necessary price for any democracy to pay. He closes with the observation that we have been freeloading militarily for some time, and so we owe these flights to "our allies."

He does not mention the fact that our allies in Germany and Britain and the USA are finding Labrador to be increasingly expensive and, in fact, are hesitating to sign the "memorandum of agreement," which will tie both Canada and its allies to continued treetop whizzing. Several other places, such as Turkey, South Africa, and even Cold Lake, Alberta, are looking more economical and may not involve the pesky annoyance of Innu protests, or their equivalent. He also does not mention that the real demand for these flights is not from war machines and/or paranoiacs but from the Newfoundland government, which is desperate for *any* industry to take root. It does not matter if the resulting plant and its poisonous fruit devastate everything they touch, so long as the planters are willing to pay. Canada is more willing to endure Innu protests at the UN and in Europe, with their sympathetic responses, than it is to have to do something real and expensive to save Newfoundland from economic collapse in this century. To hell with the caribou and the Innu, send us your jobs.

I stop for gas in Prawda, and I'm clenched with anger. Free-floating anger ranks way up there as a useless and destructive emotion, in fact probably is the main feeding source for many ugly hatreds, so I try to work against my considerable tendency to feel and indulge anger, to permit its existence.

I get out of the truck and just let the warm bright morning fold around me. It is busy at Prawda today, and the two full-service attendants are hopping. "I don't know which way to turn," says the man as cars and trucks and credit cards and windshields line up. The woman attendant on the other pump says to the half-ton trucker, who gracelessly teases her about her difficulty in reaching his windshield, "I find that I can do it." I admire her response and my anger backs off, but just to the corner.

The dissonance is still jangling loud and wrong. I worked and lived for a decade in Labrador and have a wide and deep reservoir of affection for the Innu and Settlers and Inuit, and especially for the land. To use it as a practice killing ground is obscene, especially when the tempting jobs tied to the military base are so desperately needed by those dependent on the wage economy. The employment is regionally and racially divisive, because the Innu, and to a lesser extent the Inuit, passionately oppose the military presence and all that it symbolizes and actualizes in Canada's disregard for the land, and for the centuries of regional stewardship of the land.

The recent Canadian decision to continue and increase the military flights only makes sense if we assume a malevolent, environmentally rapacious, internationally militaristic, racist, greedy beyond counting, and (the kicker) stone-stupid dominant Canadian culture. Otherwise, how can we for an instant justify these low-level flights and what they mean to a land and peoples to whom we owe so much? I just do not get it.

After gassing up my truck, and suppressing a brood regarding links between my vehicle's gas and pavement needs and the Labrador wage economy's rush "full throttle into hell's own flames," as one Labrador resident used to say, I go have a coffee. My daughter Sarah gave me a little blank notebook a couple of years ago, and I put quotes and found images in it. There is no serendipity, only linkage. Today, I leaf through it and come upon this note from a long, happy ride to Thunder Bay with a friend: "Russian poet Yevtushenko on Morningside with Gzowski, says 'a common enemy unites a people; a common victory divides them.'"

There it is. Dissonance is merely misperception, and I have been, once again, blind and slow to grasp connections. Canada is insisting on continuing this military lunacy, at great cost to its own self-image, simply to give the Innu a common enemy. This is not self-defeating Canadian insanity but instead quite the opposite, a self-sacrificing gambit, a ploy which gives the Innu a gift of unifying purpose. Small cost the caribou calving grounds and migratory routes, and small cost the absence of national pacifistic righteousness, as the aim is now clear. Let's just pretend that someone, maybe the Cape Bretoners, will rise up with sticks or even rusty shovels, and let's also pretend we may have to low-level bomb the breath out of them. The Innu will overcome our centuries of exploitation and racism by opposing all of us, their common enemy, the bombers and the bombees, *thereby increasing their unity*. Bless you, Canada; how could I have doubted?

There is one small problem, because if Yevtushenko is right, we can't let the Innu win, not ever, as this would only divide them. I drive away from Prawda, content that there's no way Canada's going to make that mistake and let the Innu win one. Not on your life, and not on theirs.

Impolite Company
(submission to the *Globe and Mail*
—no response received)

A person I work with in northwestern Ontario asked me, just before the New Year, if I had seen the TV news piece on Black Tickle, Labrador, a few weeks before. I hadn't. She described the scenes of poverty, including inadequate shelter and food, with no announcements of planned or anticipated relief. She told me because she knows I used to live in Labrador and senses that I love the place.

My first visits to the community of Black Tickle were twenty-five years ago, and as with so much of Labrador, it was a visit to another country, bringing me into contact with a new set of geographical and cultural assumptions. The town is on the Island of Ponds, partway down the south Labrador coast, and it is an offshore patch of arctic-like tundra. The houses are scattered around a narrow and deep harbour, and in the summer an independent procession of huge icebergs eases by in the Labrador current, just outside the island's hills, with nothing between their leading ice edges and Ireland but the full Atlantic. The place is spectacular.

It gets its name from either the deep, and therefore

black, run of water (a tickle) between the "mainland" (the large island) and a smaller island, or from the unusually dark lichen on the dominant rocks. It depends on whom you ask or where you look.

In the '70s and early '80s, I was lucky enough to visit Black Tickle again and again as the travelling doctor for the south Labrador coast, functioning as the nurses' assistant for the strong and caring nurse practitioners who didn't just visit; they stayed. The poverty we encountered on a daily basis was staggering, with tiny cold shacks, grossly inadequate nutrition, sparse educational and health-care resources, one bare but expensive store, few fish to be caught and sold, and with a long trip required on ski-doo to get water and firewood. It was also home, the only place they "belonged to" for generations of families of Keefes and Roberts and Dysons, descendants of emigrants from the United Kingdom a couple of hundred years ago. Moving away was not an option, not if you had grown attached to the land and water and not if your life was the life of the place.

On one winter morning, cold and blowing, a nurse-friend and I were doing house calls. We came into a frigid, tiny and drafty house, where I had to duck to avoid breaking the lightbulb out of the ceiling socket. The entire family was seated on chairs and boxes around the open oven of the electric stove. We were told that they couldn't buy oil for the furnace-stove because the welfare cheque had been cut off, and they weren't sure why. They were hungry, and there was a long winter in front of them. The phones were "out," so I just saved up my sympathy and anger, let it simmer, and when I got back to Northwest River a few days later, I called "welfare" in Goose Bay.

My message was simple: if the family I'd seen, and five

others in the same predicament we had later found, didn't receive adequate and ongoing funding by 72 hours from *now*, my next calls would be to radio, television and papers, in St. John's, Halifax, and Toronto. "They *love* a good poverty story at this time of year; nicely sets off the Christmas and New Year's optimism and largesse. We'll probably get coverage on the *National*. You might even have to explain your 'policies' to Lloyd Robertson. Are you following me, here?" He was, and the people got their cheques, and they never knew why—another random whim of the inscrutable bureaucratic gods.

Twenty-five years later, the same story, but who to call?

Stories

"I see that I must give what I most need."
—Anne Michaels,
in *Fugitive Pieces*

"...it may be in our sexuality that we are most
easily enslaved....The politics of the flesh
are the roots of power."
—Ursula K. Le Guin,
in *Four Ways to Forgiveness*

The Devil You Know

Grade 6, for some of us, carried with it a random cruelty and sense of preparation for loss that seemed to indicate an unavoidable direction, a time on a continuum.

We had two teachers that year, starting off with Miss Blain, whom we saw as simply being old and skinny and crazy. She would scream and her spit would fly, covering about a 45-degree span and up to 5 feet. (We measured.) The strap was not her chief weapon because she would start to cry before we did, usually by the second whack. Her scream was her forte, and maybe she had once known that and had manipulated her vocal range, but now she was out of control. A runaway shriek.

The toilet was her downfall after only three months of school that year, and with the usual slim years to go before her retirement. I have since learned that teachers soon become wary of refusing access to the toilet. A few wet or lumpy shorts in the memory of an elementary-school teacher, when combined with the subsequent parental rampage, produce respect for the excretory urge.

A rising stream of demands by the young gentlemen to

"leave the room," with a half-hour lull to bring on Miss Blain's inevitably disastrous false confidence, followed by a rapid-fire burst of obviously urgent evacuation requests by every male in the room, was sure to bring her to tears and occasionally get us the afternoon off. She would lean over on her desk, head on left arm, sobbing and wetting the sleeve of her ten-year-old blouse. I don't remember any of us ever revealing shame, and I don't think any of us ever thought of her as a real person.

As she began to have more and more collapses over smaller things, we were able to get the girls to join in too. We hated her weakness, her distance from everything that seemed real to us, and her spit. We were in revolt.

We never knew what happened then but simply noticed that she stopped coming to school. We noticed this casually, with true nonchalance. We didn't care.

They brought in a mercenary to smash the revolt. A curly-haired, constantly smiling man from away. Someone named a province, and we glanced at the Neilson's chocolate-bar map of Canada. The first day Mr. Gray was there, Rick put up his hand at a blatantly inappropriate time, in the middle of roll call. On being asked what he wanted, Rick marched red-faced to the front of the room, doing what he knew a good Nova Scotian must do.

"Yes, Rick?" said Gray. He had learned our names quickly, a bad sign.

"Are you staying here?" Rick asked, knowing all souls were firmly behind him but finding this a bit stiff anyway.

"Go sit down, Rick," said Gray, which was an inadvertently kind response, as Rick was stranded there and the room was very quiet. "To answer his stupid question," continued Gray after Rick had shot back to his seat, "I will only stay here if I decide that you deserve me."

Maybe we deserved each other. Mr. Gray proved to be our match, with some to spare. He was a man of games, with a playful sense of humour that was stimulated by his collection of Grade 6 malcontents.

I don't think we were a challenge for him. Our toilet ploy failed immediately, and he seemed annoyed by the simplicity of our attack. He controlled our effort by stating that each of us could "go to the washroom" once in the morning and once in the afternoon, that we had seven minutes per visit, and that we were to stay in after school to make up all Toilet Time, which he carefully recorded on the front board. We drank extra at the white enamel fountain that always had warm water, hoping to embarrass him with a disaster. We hadn't decided who would make this ultimate sacrifice, but by Grade 6 the sphincters are firmed up more than adequately and we stayed dry in our seats.

Gray enjoyed his time in school, inventing new games. The strap was used for anything and on anyone. Girls were not exempt, the star pupil of the class was not exempt, and the pre-jocks and hard cases were not singled out enough to give them special status. Rick was strapped, hard, for dropping his pencil—we got the message. He strapped Amy, with her red hair and big glasses and marks of 98, for misspelling a word. There was a strange surprise on her face as the strap actually hit her hand, leaving it red and shaking.

Mr. Gray knew that if you strapped too hard the hand went numb, and he definitely didn't want that. He was a medium-weight, slow-speed strapper, the worst kind. He would watch our faces, and smile, and invent new reasons for strapping every day. But hands harden, and all of us, Amy included, got so that we could just stand and not move our hands or change our expression or flinch when he faked a hit and then winged by the hand, laughing. ("A better deker than Gordie Howe," some kid said.) After a few weeks, he tired of the strap as entertainment, maintaining random use for its deterrent value.

Gray soon found that the one thing we all wanted, unanimously and unceasingly, was to get out of school. So, in the afternoon, after the final bell and with the sound of other classes leaving the building as a background, he would play the question game. He would ask, "How many want to leave?" and, if most people put up their hands, he would allow the others to go, the ones with their hands down, saying they should be rewarded for their willingness to stay in school. After a five-minute wait, the question would be "How many want to go to the movie?" and if the minority put up hands, he would let them out, saying he wouldn't want them to be late. (We called the movie "the show," and it played every afternoon after school, for 15 cents.) Gray usually, but not always, picked the smallest number, hands-up or hands-down. Some of us would sit for a half-hour most days. We were his favourites, and he loved to play with us.

Gerry Aldon was in our class. He was tall, about two inches over Gray and a good six inches over the rest of us, having "failed" two years along the way. He wore a short army jacket, winter and summer, and was rough. Gerry enjoyed putting tacks on seats and giving hard jabs to the belly, depending on his mood and the audience to stimulate his game plan. He was the undisputed lion of the class and no one pushed him. Gray cruised around Gerry's periphery a bit, making occasional attacks with the strap and keeping him in even when he knew Gerry was going to the show, but not very often. That much muscle and so little brain must be dangerous, or so we'd all been taught, even Gray.

I made the basic mistake of talking to my father about Gerry. I don't know what led to this atypical moment of familial confidence sharing, probably just a weak moment in which I forgot that parents need to be protected from children's realities. Dad told me, slowly because I was only in Grade 6, that bullies are always cowards and if anyone, small or big, terrified or not, challenges a bully he runs away. Guaranteed.

I knew it was no good, but I made a last-ditch effort to counter my father's advice by telling of Gerry's good qualities such as his kindness to his deaf sister, whom I invented, and his usefulness at breaking a path to school in blizzards. Dad was only moved to advise me not to be too hard on him in future fistic encounters.

I was now armed with my father's advice and so was invincible—the dream of every scrawny Grade 6 pacifist when faced with Gerry Aldon. The obvious question, which haunts me now, is why didn't I ignore the advice? I was 12 years old, and my father was my father, and in a way that is the only answer. I had been told what I had to do, and it simply didn't occur to me to do anything else.

During the unusual exchange of father-son world views, I had carefully avoided mentioning Gerry's actual usefulness, or so we saw it, in keeping adults such as Gray under control. We all feared Gray much more than Gerry. "The devil you know . . ." was a rule we were comfortable with. We felt that Gerry acted as a visual brake on Gray, and we cherished the possibility of Gerry becoming annoyed by one of Gray's surges of humour, lifting him up and throwing him through the closed window of our second-storey classroom onto the paved school yard.

Gerry said he would do it for $10 and laughed his eyes-rolled-up, deep-voiced cackle.

I was at this time, Grades 5 to 8 to be exact, a reliable homing target for bullies, potential or aspiring bullies, and bullies' victims who were stronger than I was. So Gerry and I knew each other fairly well, and even though I was usually horizontal in this relationship, or impaled on a needle he brought to school with him one entire winter, we also occasionally talked.

Gerry Aldon was lonely and without hope, and I saw this, and he knew that I knew. I didn't feel the urge to secretly mock him, and he knew that too. My sole request was that he leave me be, a simple thought, carefully worded.

We occasionally went together to the afternoon movie at Randy Wentzell's theatre. Gerry would talk in the anonymity of the dark, nudging me with his elbow at a kissing scene or a particularly elegant killing. Leaving the movie, he would never speak as he turned to go home. If we were alone, I would casually say, "See you tomorrow," but would say nothing if others were around.

Gerry was, therefore, surprised and hurt one morning, soon after my talk with my father, when I apparently took real offense at his having dented my shin with his army boot and responded by kicking back and saying loudly that I wanted to see him at recess. "Seeing" meant fighting. Gerry and the others who had heard looked at me in amazed silence, aware that I had become totally unhinged overnight. Gerry's face showed that I would unfortunately have to be done away with. I was terrified and hoped I wouldn't faint or wet myself *before* he hit me. Gerry sulked for the rest of the hour, not bothering to torment a single person.

Mr. Gray had seen the exchange. At recess, I went outside wondering what it was I was really supposed to *do* here. When I got to the fighting place, behind the school and out of sight of the teachers' cigarette and coffee room at the front of the building, I turned around to see Gerry coming, slowly. Gray was there too, further back, hanging close to the corner of the building. Gerry walked up to me, and before I could start to swing, he cuffed me on the side of the head with the palm of his hand, knocking me over, and then started to walk away. He had looked truly sad, although he had often hit me much harder than that as part of his daily rounds. I was up very quickly, nothing if not fast, and tackled him behind the knees. Gerry went down, hitting his head on the building and opening a cut over his eye. As he got up, looking confused and with blood running down his face, I was at him, crying and swinging and kicking and yelling, wanting to kill him, to somehow make up for the Blains and Grays and fathers, and even for Gerry Aldon. I don't think I actually hit him, but I remember Gerry pushing me down to the ground and being poised over me with his fist in the air. He didn't swing it down, and my opinion varies with the time of my life as to whether or not he would have.

He didn't get the chance, or at least the chance was deflected. Gray came up from behind and grabbed Gerry's arm, too quickly and much too hard. Gerry threw him against the wall and hit him full in the face with his fist and then in the abdomen. Gray crumpled, bleeding. Gerry looked at me, and I was afraid for a second that he was going to cry. Then he went home.

Gerry was expelled, and I didn't sit with him anymore during movies. He didn't touch me or speak to me again. Gray was quieter, having perhaps heard the cheers when Gerry hit him.

My father never did ask again about Gerry, and I've wondered occasionally if he heard of the thing and if he was proud or ashamed, but it's more likely that he simply forgot all about our talk. A trivial and unremarkable event, a mere transferring of truths about bullies.

While it was all too clear in Grade 6 that this life is particularly unfit for living, that was also the beginning of a very dangerous time when it was not yet known that there is another side to even that coin.

Three to Dance

The first day I heard of Ross was the first day I truly knew of you, actually saw you. The four of us, The Foursome we called ourselves, using capital letters with our one voice, drove by the house. It looked old and ordinary, in an ordinary way. Maybe no one lived in it, hard to tell. It was a dirty yellow colour with curved windows in those wooden turrets. It was on a hill, and it was big.

We could see the cove from there, where the water emptied all the way out and left only mud; low tide.

The windows were dark with something across them, but not curtains. The lawn was deep, good for the animals we didn't have, with trees, and a hedge that might allow us a place to be naked if we felt like it. We had driven around much of the province trying to find it, calmly, but urgently needing to find a place where we would have a chance to become real. All of us felt that we would have to try something new and difficult or we couldn't last. But one or two or maybe all of us also needed to watch our unity explode, needed to find that every house was already lived in. We were afraid. So we touched each other and talked loudly about what we would build the rooms to be, and how keeping any kids we had out of school would be easier in an isolated area like this, and how we could help them freely learn anything they wanted to know, but none of us knew how a grasshopper cried.

We ignored that and others, and talked and talked, about trying and changing, beating jealousies and in-securities. We also needed to beat hope, and probably hate, but we didn't mention these.

We drove up a yard, a driveway that bumped and made us walk, helped us walk. The afternoon was warm, that new time when the leaves are lettuce green but limp and fragile and one is forced to hope they will flatten out and harden.

The man and woman at the house accepted us easily, asked us in, a grey-winded old house without paint, with the musty remembering smell of aging photographs. Only the two of them, old to us, they accepted our manner of being and we accepted theirs, neither changing a single step.

We were in their kitchen, and it seemed to us to be expanding, this full feeling due to people asking us in and seeming to care enough to give food and time. We ignored the possibility of custom; we were always ignoring things. And we asked them about the house, eagerly; or wanting to be. They told about Ross.

I didn't get the family history straight, so I'll just leave it. The main thing is that Ross and his mother lived alone in the house. It's a big house, with a lot of high, small windows that are difficult to look out of, and an upstairs, and a steep roof. We knew that the house was ours.

The mother had been caught up and overrun with the idea of clean. The children, Ross and the others, had always been straightened and pressed for school or

Saturday or anything. Games weren't allowed because games had sweat and dirt and were loud. When she came home from work and the still young kids would run to hug her, she would tell them not to touch until she washed. A father was never mentioned, and none of us thought to ask. That seems strange, and I don't know why we didn't. It didn't seem to be important.

All of the children eventually left for jobs or marriages or a city, except Ross. He took over a room in the basement while his mother used the rest of the house for herself, all ten rooms. People driving by the house at night, late, would see her through a window, washing walls, windows, everything. Ross had his room and she never went there, just left it for him to look after, but he couldn't use any part of the upper house without cleaning up after.

As she got older the mother got more and more involved with this idea of keeping the house clean, to the point where Ross wasn't allowed to eat, wash, sit, void, or do anything upstairs except pass through it to get to the basement, and quickly. Before she died the mother began to accuse Ross of keeping whores in the basement and defiling her house with his presence. She made him hold his breath as he walked through.

The old man told us that the mother had died about five years before and that Ross was living alone in the house now. He was near 35 years old, a skilled carpenter, mechanic, and fisherman who charged huge fees and didn't care if you hired him or not, had never been seen with a woman or a man, had an old mongrel car he had made from bits, and his body odour was renowned. The man said he knew Ross and would show us the house, since Ross was away. He smiled.

We got in our car, the old man bringing his own, not

51

saying why, and we followed him. We were quiet; both cars right into the yard, the feeling of not having a right to be there. The old man said he thought the women might be particularly interested in the kitchen, so we would go in the back door. The porch had holes between some boards, and we were careful, but the door was stuck. He banged it open with his arm and let us go in first, probably so he could watch.

There was rotting garbage on every inch of the floor, empty piled boxes, the heads of chickens, and the sharp smell of urine. The stove had pots on it with something thick left in them and a black tar over all of it. The room was dark because sacking had been nailed over the windows. The man pointed to the clogged sink with garbage and urine in it, and then to feces on the floor. Cath vomited. That strikes me now as being due to guilt or relief, since she probably wanted our houses to fall down more than anyone else did. Maybe it was guilt at knowing she was glad, that this really was our house. More than eight sides to a triangle, always.

The old man led the rest of us on. His attitude was strange. He was enjoying himself. Maybe he disliked us, but probably it was much simpler than that. The next room was where Ross spent most of his time. A lot of furniture was in the room, at angles, ornaments unmoved and undusted on the mantle, an inch of dust everywhere, more sacking over the window, garbage, no urine or feces, a TV tube with no casing, boxes; a dark room, and we couldn't find a light. He then took us into a relatively immaculate "parlour," thick with dust but completely in order, with curtains in place and old upholstered furniture. Maybe it had been beautiful. The upstairs was the same. Ross hadn't reached these rooms, yet. We left.

Fifteen years later I came back. I had to. The feeling is a nagging one of things unfinished, a hand almost held. Similar to the need to touch someone you think could be a part of your life, just to have it made certain one way or the other. There is almost a relief when the person rejects the touch, or doesn't know it happened, because you are free from the doubt, the possibility. The worst thing in my life is a step being left not taken because of that need for security. I can only stand myself if I either make it happen or destroy the potential. So I came back.

I went to the old people's house, but they were dead. Then I looked until I found a person who would talk and also knew, down by the weir. Through the time I had been thinking Ross had been urinating on his mother's head, drop by drop, but it had been more than that. His mother had had her will changed just before she died, when Ross had all those whores in his bachelor's cellar, and had left the house to Ross's brothers with the stipulation that Ross be allowed to live there as long as he wished. Ross had wanted the house and had pleaded, explained, but no one changed, the way people don't.

In the ten years after we saw it, Ross had gone from room to room, living there, but never combing his shed skins together. They were everywhere. His bathroom was the room he had last lived in. Then he left. Two brothers came to the house, went in, came out and drove away. No one had been in the house since.

I drove by the house again, desperately needing to remove all trace of The Foursome from myself, but unable to.

I then tried to write the brothers about buying the house, but the letters were returned. I was also unable to contact Ross. No one knew, or cared, where he was. It was only known that he had spent fifteen years of his life, his time, alone in the house, and then left. So we came back, together.

As we stand looking at the huge old dead house, I can not escape the feeling that Ross has done us a favour. All these years later, we seem to agree on this, the two of us, as we walk away, not talking.

Wind Toys, Again

Tomorrow is my birthday.

It's getting late, the wind is blowing, and I'm sitting here hoping that Cath avoids being cruel tomorrow. We have been giving each other increasingly elaborate gifts over the last two years since we moved to the Arctic and met Anton. I think of these gifts, including my choices, as being desperate, superstitious even, attempting to ward off inevitable pain. It would be particularly destructive if Cath were to buy me another of Anton's miniature carvings. That would move us into a whole new phase. This has to happen, but not yet.

"Where are you going? Do you know what *time* it is?" Cath doesn't look right at me.

"For a walk. I might even go into Anton's, if his light's on."

Silence. A friend, not Anton, recently said that relationships consist of islands of silence of increasing size. I didn't believe him.

I leave the house, thinking of what Cath and I are doing and of what we're undoing, as I lean into the gale and it pushes at me, plays with me. The trick in the flat Arctic wind is to not argue with it, to empty yourself of fear and thought and fight, simply to go along, even when it's blowing right into you. Another island of silence, only this time it's your own, and it is comforting.

Anton's lights are on, all of them, it seems. I go in, not knocking; we're past the polite stage.

"What do you want?" he says. He's bent over a minia-ture carving of three polar bears, two adults and a cub, coming up on a seal behind a low ice ridge, all of this set on a rough irregular piece of bone the size of his palm, smaller even. The bears and seal are white, emerging from ivory. The seal has a life expectancy of one minute at most, but it's all frozen. This seal will go on waiting, unaware.

"Just out walking, following the wind. Saw your light. I still feel comfortable here, in spite of everything. And I *do* love your work; the size is so appropriate."

"My *work*! Toys for whites, just like us. Why don't you go home."

"I'm going. That's a fine piece. My sympathy is with the seal, you know. Why are you up so late?"

"Mine isn't; the seal deserves what it gets. It's careless." Looking at me now, smiling the old smile, maybe with kindness, I can't tell. "Someone wants this done by tomor-row, and I've been putting it off. You should go home."

The wind is on my back as I leave, and it's really howl-ing now; out of control is how it sounds.

When I come into the house, one light has been left on in the living room. I go to the bookcase and find Richard Brautigan's *In Watermelon Sugar*, needing the brutal whimsy of his view and wishing he hadn't killed himself. A little perspective might have helped. I find the passage I'm looking for:

...the wind was blowing harder and harder
now and a few small things fell down.

I put on my coat and go back out.

Private Joke

There was some time, just after I had found shelter in the Arctic but then decided to leave, when the Maritime road was a casual warm place to be. It was good to be alone, or so it seemed. I have always known roads better than any face, and the problems of disappointment and acceptance don't usually intrude on a slow solitary walk up a blind hill.

My rules were simpler then. They were part of my equipment, my pack, and they changed with the mood and the urgency, and with the angle of the weather. Hitching at night was to be avoided, as no one knew you were there and neither did you. Walking was the only sure way to feel connected, but if it were a long trip, or if moving took you away from the carefully picked standing-spot where the long-distance trucks had to slow, then it couldn't be afforded. More often, it would simply happen that the excuse for standing out there was irrelevant. On these days, you would walk mile after mile and a car was an intrusion. When you are on foot, the bridges and ditches are louder; they can be heard.

On one melting afternoon in March I was in a hurry

to cross distance and so picked a clear spot to wait. There was room for a car to pull over but not a truck. Sometimes, not having the possibility of both didn't seem important. I had on the proper hitchhiker's stance and clothes and face, not malignant or too eager or annoyingly nonchalant, but just this side of invisible. Parents would even ask me to hold their children when I was like this, and they had guessed right.

This day, early afternoon, a social worker asked me to hold the child she was saving from a bad home so as to be given a haunted future. I held him as gently as possible and tried to move him away from fear and into sleep by not intruding and by letting him sense the harmless space around my eyes. He did sleep. After a while, the social worker looked over at me, at us, and said, "You're wasting your time; he doesn't know you're there. He's not normal." The child woke up soon after that, and I left them so I could walk and be alone.

I was damn near gleeful when I left that car, in spite of what I'd seen in the kid's face, because the hateful social worker had put her finger right on it. If you're not normal, don't waste your time. Just get out of it, back away, leave the game.

This was one of the happiest and most dangerous days of my life. We all have these days, when you *feel* the lightning gathering to hit and yet you just rise taller to meet it and shake your fist at the high, and laugh. You have to hope you get these days, and you have to pray they don't come very often.

That summer was a time when I was trying to make sense of things, of all the things, small and big, and as a result I was getting the impression that life itself is not normal, not able to be lived in a sane way. I still think I was on to something there, but the danger lay in the fact that I had yet to see, to feel, the balancing sense of joy, in a consistent sustaining way that I recognized and could retain. When the social worker spoke to me, I gave up and went looking for my way out.

I walked all afternoon, and I got lucky, as some of us do. It was a simple thing; I must have come too close to a bird's nest or come up too quietly, something. This bird, just a little one, flew right at my head, over and over, chirping its feathered ass off, madder than hell. I took off, running hard, and looked back to see it circling, victorious. That bird suddenly seemed normal to me, fighting to hold on to life. It had thrown me a line.

Later, just before dark, a car pulled over with a mud-flying, brakes-jammed stop that meant we might pass on hills. An army ant sat gripping the wheel, and while he talked I sat my hitchhiker role of listening and appearing to agree, just barely there but enough for him. The sun went into the hood, very red, helping us through the Wentworth Valley, and he was silent for a while. Then it was dark and Army got lonely again and talked.

While in Puerto Rico he had learned a truth, and this truth was a trick. Some of the people would catch a scorpion, spread lighter fluid in a circle around it and light the fluid. On seeing the flames, the bright heat without sign of relief, the scorpion would quickly swing the barbed tail up over its back and into its own head, just behind the eyes, and immediately die. With other scorpions wider circles of flame were drawn, just to see what would happen. I forget the measurements but at a certain point the scorpion would freeze and wait for the flame to go away, instinctively rejecting the suicide plan. They would then kill it with a stick.

Our speed in the car had not altered and I flinched in the quiet darkness when the first large truck met and passed us without Army driving straight into it. Apparently, our circle had an exit and, even more importantly, I was glad it did.

Army commented, after miles of silence, that it was a funny way to get a piece of tail, but he didn't laugh and I didn't feel it was necessary for me to do so either.

Jailbirds

She is thinking of leaving. Just getting to this point has been more difficult and frightening than she expected. She has tried going to a counsellor, to find out why the mere thought of leaving should scare her so deeply. She had often entertained other, far worse ideas before, without fear or shame. She assumes everyone has done this, more or less, with the tones and twists of their fantasies being influenced by wit and experience, but not caused by them. The fear is new.

The counsellor, a quick, detached, stylish woman of her own age, had all too rapidly sized her up and pronounced that the depth of her fear was based on potential for loss-of-sense-of-self. She, the counsellor, said that our identities are tied up in ritual and persistence in our roles, and that if these are abandoned or stolen, the person becomes stuck with fear. "What you're contemplating is leaving yourself," was how she put it, with a wave of warmth pushing past the professional distance and matching earrings. The counsellor wanted her to talk more, much more, about her other fantasies and thoughts. Even though there was a possibility that they were getting somewhere, they didn't really recognize or like each other, so the sessions stopped.

However, the point had been made, and clearly. So as she gets ready to go out for her daily ten-kilometre walk, she tries to figure out not only what she *wants* to do, but what she *has* to do.

There are worse fates, she thinks, than tying one's sense-of-self to rituals and roles, and to prove the point she rapidly ticks off several worse fates. Now, all I've got to do is find some new pictures of myself, she thinks, as she pulls on a T-shirt and jogging shorts. Thank God for small breasts, she again concludes, happy with not having to bother to hide or contain them on her running-walks. She stands at the mirror, to see if the reflected eyes hold direction. They don't.

She gets ready to go into the hall from the second-floor apartment, pausing at the door with her sneakers in her hand. It has been several years since there have been neighbours this close, where she can hear a sneeze, or a phone ring. Occasionally, she can also hear anger or love, usually more muted but definite. I've spent about fifteen years of my life in apartments, she thinks, remembering her childhood home and her parents. It feels familiar and comfortable, like moving next door to someone you grew up with, who knows more about you than they should, but not too much more. It is acceptable.

One of the apartment neighbours is sick, with a chronic, progressive illness that is leading to weight loss and insomnia and staying at home. They don't know each other and don't speak, but the signs are there to be seen by watchful neighbours. I haven't found a way to help, she thinks, and then realizes that maybe she hasn't looked for one.

She goes out to the hallway and sits on the steps which go from the second floor to the top floor, lacing up her sneakers for the walk which she intends to be gruelling, sweaty and exhausting, on this very hot mid-July day. Up the building's steps comes the Meals-on-Wheels' happy whistler, and she's been able to hear him all the way from the parking lot, a steady high-volume version of some Sound-of-Music-like semi-tune. This is someone who is determined to be happy. Meals-on-Wheels comes once a day, bringing food to the sick neighbour in small hard plastic containers, which they retrieve the following noon when they bring the next meal. The whistler is in his late sixties or older, and he's puffing as he comes up the steep two flights, still whistling between puffs. He is not going to let the cheery side down. He's startled to see her sitting there lacing up her sneakers, but quickly recovers and they exchange the obligatory Canadian nice-day-hot-but-we'd-die-for-this-in-February pleasantries.

As she goes down the stairs, tightly laced, she hears Mr. Julie Andrews trying to rouse her neighbour who sleeps during the hot days and is up at night. Her own night-time wandering has revealed this, and she has been intrigued to hear tapes of Second World War news broadcasts coming through the wall from his living room at 3 am, as the Allied Forces gain a toe-hold in Italy and victory is finally a possibility.

She pauses on reaching the bottom steps, before going out into the noon heat, waiting for the conclusion, and finally hears her neighbour open the door. She's relieved; yet another life saved by a hot meal and a moderately well-whistled show tune. Her own contribution requires review; later.

For now there is the walk, only the walk. She has

found, or created, the loop, a ten-kilometre rambling
circle that usually takes her about ninety minutes. It starts
from beside the lake and goes through the park, then down
to the main highway before avoiding that traffic by taking
curving side-street routes, including the high walking-
bridge over the railroad tracks. Sometimes there are
people drinking up there, in the breeze and above the
trains, and she usually stops to say hello, with direct and
calm eye contact, but only for a few seconds. "Nice legs,"
one said the other day, grinning; harmless, she thinks. She
just waved over her shoulder, a thank-you wave, and kept
going, not too fast, not too slow. Her route will then take
her up and down a couple of hills, along the curving busy
harbourfront, and up the last hill to home, back to the
apartment.

On this very hot day she has walked slowly, and is
winding down her pace even more as she goes along the
sidewalk approaching the railroad underpass just before
the harbourfront, "the subway," it is called. Several cars
and trucks are lined up for the light. A man leans out of his
pick-up truck driver's window and shouts at the small car
stopped in front of him, "Hey, jailbird," then louder and
more harshly, "HEY! JAILBIRD! How do you like it outside?" She is walking quite close to both car and truck, as
the road narrows for the underpass. It seems to her that
everything slows at this point, the vehicles and the sounds,
her walking, all of it converges. In the small car, still waiting for a green light, a woman in the back seat leans
forward and puts a hand on the shoulder of the man who
is at the wheel, the jailbird. Both the driver and the comforting back-seat woman look to be about her age, she
thinks as she watches them from only a few feet away. How
can that be? she thinks. How can they be able to share

this? The jailbird is staring ahead, grim, holding the wheel with both hands, but it is obvious that he too felt the hand on his shoulder, and has accepted it. The light changes and all vehicles move on. Everything resumes normal speed, as the small car and the pick-up truck go the same way, to the west.

There is a cooling breeze coming off the lake into the apartment as she enters. She hadn't wanted to lug keys along on the walk and so just left the door open, as usual. The apartment feels safer, less confining. She considers the possibility of having the door unlocked all night, all the time, if she stays. The fear of leaving has eased, now that she sees it as a possibility and not a necessity.

Travels

"These were just some
of the things I saw as I passed
through delusion and ignorance
and fear: those were the various
states of grace allowed to me
in my small life."

—Catherine Hunter,
in *Latent Heat*

"... there's a certain pattern that emerges when
you observe something long enough."

—Jackie Johnson Maughan,
in *Go Tell it on the Mountain*

"... I see the patterns. When you see
the patterns you tend to be afraid ..."

—Greg Hollingshead,
in *The Roaring Girl*

Don Quixote at the Holiday Inn

The University of Manitoba's Community Medicine (public health) specialists-in-training get a chance to tour the nearby nuclear plant every year, as an excursion into the real world of occupational and environmental health. (The possibility of an intrinsic conflict of aims between our jobs and the ecosystem *has* occurred to us.)

Five of us drive through Manitoba's late-winter fields of snow for over two hours, watching the world move itself from prairie to Canadian Shield. A nuclear-power referendum conducted in this car would probably come out 3 to 2 against. My contention is that nuclear power is less exploitive and destructive of First Nations'/northern lands than the present hydroelectric dams and their flooding, and less harmful to our short-term ecosystem than are oil and gas and coal. I suggest to my travelling public-health colleagues, a politically centrist and slightly-maybe-sometimes-left group that we roll the long-term environmental dice, placing present-day First Nations' interests ahead of all of our great-grandchildren's, and take our chances. I'm pummelled with incredulous

choruses of the "you-*must*-be-kidding" variety, question-
ing my logic, sanity, environmental goodwill, and political
leftness, in no particular order. I'm amazed that my DMM
(dreadful macho maleness) does not get cited as a causal
factor for my wrongheadedness, and I voice this amaze-
ment, with my usual calm restraint. The vote switches to 4
to 1 against.

There is no safe place to hide at 8:00 am in a crowded
car when the temperature, speed, radio-station choices,
politics, and conversational accoutrements do not satisfy
anyone for longer than fifteen minutes at a stretch. We are
able, however, to reach a rapid all-party agreement on our
shared need to get back to the city early. We have different reasons for this need. A guest speaker is coming to the
Holiday Inn, and I have a ticket but keep this fact to
myself. Once pummelled, twice quiet—sometimes.

✳ ✳ ✳

During the five-hour tour-plus-lunch, we are all relatively
subdued, an unusual state for this crowd. It is difficult to
pinpoint the cause of the mood. We are sufficiently aware
of the contradictions present in the societal energy debate
that our defense of individual biases lacks that self-
righteous fervor so common to specialists of any stripe.
We are uncertain.

There is also a wearying Alice in Sillyland aura to our
tour of this plant, enhanced by the cheerful, self-assured,
technological mumbo jumbo of the staff, the ostentatious
"safety" measures including identity badges and protective
clothing and glowing water baths for the radioactive
STUFF, and a sharp awareness that we are shut deep inside
on a day that has maybe become sunny and springtime

warm. We don't know *what* the weather is out there in the world. We have been shrunk. We are Alice.

The tour guides keep us moving, long jaunts along stairs and hallways, whipping unfazed past Geiger counters, which seem to be clicking away at anything that stirs, past a shiny, tidy library where two people in postures of improvisational abandonment are rooting away amidst piles of printed words, and past new wings and old generators. All the while we're trying to sense what is really going on here. Each one of us, in our own way, is trying to fingertip the necessary-evil strong points and the eventually deadly Achilles' heels. As we traipse along yet another underground passageway, I'm reminded of the aging parents' rule of "slow them down by keeping them moving." We keep moving, and we don't come anywhere near approaching the question of future-generational, cost-benefit trade-offs, not even regarding the obvious in-your-face-and-genes issue of waste disposal. We're merely tourists, hungry, tired, worried, and anxious to get home. Or, to be less generous to ourselves, we're too hip-deep in science worship and societal elitism to even consider challenging this house of cards, particularly not when we're on the verge of being admitted to the main game.

✻ ✻ ✻

On the way home, in the middle of an enthusiastic recommendation by one front-seat rider for the "subtle social commentary" present in the movie "Texas Chainsaw Massacre," another passenger talks to me of Don Quixote's scheduled visit for tonight at a disarmament conference in Winnipeg. I've got a ticket for this visit but am too far into the topic before I can admit this. (What the hell—I'll just pretend I cadged a last-minute bleacher seat from a scalper outside the Holiday Inn.) I'm an admirer of DonQ's from afar, including his politics, his partner, his hair, and his conversations with Peter Gzowski. I even like his overblown prose and have almost managed to start seeing the UN, where he is an Ambassador, as something other than a pompous, ineffectual, self-serving comic opera.

A Tory friend and I regularly exchange alien-to-alien political postcards, his drifting in from that foggy offshore island that Fats Domino affectionately called "My Blue Heaven." I vote sort-of-left, am deeply proud of having never voted for a winning candidate in 33 years of elections, and feel that DonQ proved his brilliance by not lockstepping his way through university, not even once. When the Conservatives appointed DonQ to the UN, I was amazed by the daring astuteness of the move and by its good humour, gleefully witnessing a triumph of sense over ideology. My mea culpa phone call to my Tory friend was somewhat muffled by the crow feathers in my mouth.

On CBC, DonQ assured Gzowski that he would continue to follow his own line of thought and would also continue ("usually") to say exactly what he meant. Judging by the newspaper and radio bits I get, from as safe a distance as I can attain from the charms of New York, he actually seemed to be pulling it off. There had been no resignations, no articulate public pouting, and he was damn near *gracious* when talking about the Conservatives. I very much wanted to do a radar scan on Q, his speech and expressions and posture, his current hat size and style, any reflexes that might spontaneously flick into view, and above all his heart, his centre. That seat in the Holiday Inn ballroom, back row left, had my name on it.

✳ ✳ ✳

My other reason to attend DonQ's talk was less personal and more urgent. The Canadian government, which now boasts DonQ as a paid employee, is trying to sell the NATO countries on Labrador as an on-going site for a low-level fighter aircraft training base, complete with weapons and "equipment" testing. Europe won't tolerate this type of activity over its citizens' foreheads, nor will the inhabitants of Arizona and Nevada, and what is Labrador anyway except a barren chunk of spruce-dotted taiga and granite, where only a few "native" people would care (or dare) to live? The land God gave to Cain, so what odds, let's give it back, in noise-blasted fragments.

This low-level base would mean millions of dollars to an area where employment is the exception, and jokes about the car wash closing because the person with the car moved away are the rule. The base will lead to jobs, in short, and a lot of them, for Settlers, Innu, Inuit, Newfoundlanders, mainlanders, insiders and outsiders, and for those for and against the "development"; the whole world will be able to get a job in Goose Bay, Labrador. This is the gospel according to the Chamber of Commerce, doled out by the price-of-progress-must-be-paid zealots. I, on the directly opposite hand, belong to the group that believes the price to be much too high. We are in the minority but perhaps not on this night, from the cushioned vantage point of the Holiday Inn. I plan to buttonhole DonQ, Ambassador-at-large, in hopes of stimulating his huge intellect, ego, and influence, leading him to shout, "I, Don Quixote, will not allow this ethnocentric injustice, this cultural blasphemy, to persist," something like that. DonQ will probably use much larger words and include a relevant historical reference; the rhetoric will be his choice.

＊ ＊ ＊

When I get to the Holiday Inn, the disarmament conference banquet is going on full swing behind closed doors, with a few of us DonQ groupies perched in the carpeted hall outside, waiting to be let in for the talk. After a while we are shown into a closed-off, back portion of the banquet area, with a folding wall in place between us and the real antifighters. We can hear the dessert being spooned and the coffee being slurped as we poor few spread out amongst some bare and backward tables, glancing at the sheets of disarmament announcements and opinions an aide has put in front of us. I am at a table by myself, cursing my ineptitude in not bringing any anti-NATO-base-in-Labrador tracts with me. A proselytizing opportunity missed is a convert lost.

After a wait of about 20 minutes, the wall gets folded aside, and we join the banquet. The MC gives a witty and irreverent stall-for-time rambling monologue about tangential this and that, including an explanation of the whereabouts of DonQ. He has been delayed at the airport. Then, suddenly but somewhat nonchalantly and anticlimactically, DonQ walks in, doesn't stride or amble, just walks, as if to say, "How was supper, anyway? Sorry I missed it—had some paper work to do." He looks so tired and pale, helplessly exhausted, as if whatever it is he's doing here should be cancelled; as if he and we made a mistake. A chosen-for-the-job speaker gives an embarrassingly obsequious introduction, which leads me to expect doves to whirl up out of DonQ's armpits, or for him just to put his head down and cry.

Doves don't erupt, and neither does DonQ. He adjusts his glasses and thanks the introducer with not even a hint of irony as he skips over the cotton-candy-cloud of praise. It scares the hell out of me. What if DonQ, windmill-basher extraordinaire, is keen to be hailed and stroked? The what-ifs seem to lose again this night, as Q delivers a masterful show. He seems to gain energy and colour right before our eyes, an inner recharging, as he guides us through topics and moods without revealing effort or pur-pose. We're witnessing charisma in action, a master manipulator in full flight; all we can do is hope we're not being led astray.

We are helped to feel personally reduced by the recent death of a prominent socialist, and many wipe away tears as DonQ eloquently mourns the person he admits he barely knew, but there is no evidence of opportunistic insincerity, quite the opposite. We are instead given per-mission to be emotionally attached to the *idea* of a person. Even the most hardened antiworshipers amongst us are pressed to find false emotion in DonQ's tone or words. He means what he says, and if in this plugged-septic-tank of a world it should ever turn out that he doesn't, then *we* will mean what he said; we'll have to.

It seems that very few people can sense and then convey the hint of true depth, as if these rare ones are somehow aware of the universal cobweb, the poor bastards, as well as the spider drooling its way toward them. Whether DonQ is the spider or the fly is debatable, but few who listen to him this evening would doubt his connection to the web. He takes us through an earnest defense of the UN, and not a single one of us nods off into our napkins or even flings a drying bread roll, indeed not. Jokes are scattered throughout his talk, and the weave and fluctuation of mood is fascinating to watch and to experience. The humour is humanistic, funny and respectful, and the recalled incidents he uses to illustrate his points feel relevant to our lives. His references to the politically powerful and famous contain just enough awe and respect to spare him any accusation of name-dropping or grandstanding but enough nonchalance to spare us the spectacle of an overwhelmed, subservient local product. We are witnessing a spontaneous tight-rope-walking performance, as DonQ himself strings the rope over the crowded tables, leaps up on it, adjusts his glasses and, without tumbling into anyone's water glass, makes us laugh and cry, and hope, and (almost) believe. This is not a good century to create believers, and I admire him for not even trying.

Things end abruptly, with DonQ answering a few questions but in lengthy fashion as he holds on to the rotund, speech-making tone, volume, and depth of response, unable or unwilling to let it go. Very few get to ask questions or offer challenges, but perhaps that is also part of the script. I don't get anywhere near the microphone or near DonQ after it's over. My plea for Labrador is left unsaid, stuck in my throat, and I'm reduced to hoping he knows and cares. It's been so entertaining, though, for a genuine sports fan, that I cannot work up a significant head of guilt or depression at having missed an advocacy opportunity.

When I go home and back to work, for the next several weeks images flick into my internal view, seemingly from nowhere. I experience connected images of DonQ adjusting his glasses, of nuclear windmills, Labrador river valleys and lakes, sudden snowstorms that reduce visibility beyond all reasonable expectations, and of Tolkien-like confrontations of polar opposites. Unbidden images bubbling up from the memory ponds are not subtle.

I also play an old Morningside CBC radio tape over and over, searching for clues, trying to see if Gzowski got anywhere in trying to find out if Don Quixote had sold out to the windmill, or was just coming at it from a different angle, or if the whole duel had been rigged right from the start. Even Gzowski gets nowhere on this one, and I have to admit to myself that I'm relieved he doesn't. Honesty and truth have their limits.

Move over, DonQ; we *all* are the windmill.

I'm Not Leaving
Here Forever

It's Sunday afternoon in July, at the Winnipeg Folk Festival, at Birds Hill Park, about 25 km north of Winnipeg, and I'm trying to braid my daughter's hair. This is not a full-bodied, single braid I'm trying to make but instead tiny thin ones that start at the scalp and hang straight down. I can't do it.

It is a hot afternoon and the Festival park grounds are full with more than 10,000 people wandering from one small stage of music to another, then to the food stalls, and then to the tarps spread out in front of the now empty Main Stage. These ground sheets and blankets, hundreds of them, are left in place during the day when only the small stages have music, used as a resting and meeting spot until the evening, when Main Stage comes alive.

I prefer the afternoon. People get to sit closer to the music and seem to focus, to enjoy listening and watching and talking, in a relaxed way. The Main Stage in the evening is more distant, ritualistic, a thing we have to do because it's there. The "workshops," as the shorter sessions in the afternoon are called, go on at four numbered stages and at Shady Grove and at another one called Under the Canvas in the crafts-area Home Made Village, and these are more personal and much more spontaneous. They are casual, not so much a scripted performance, or so they feel. They are also chosen in that if you don't like the music, or sitting on the grass, or the angle of the sun at Stage 2, then you can wander over to Shady Grove or just go get something to eat at the food village. It's your call, your afternoon.

My kids love the Whales' Tails—crisp, hot, pancake-size pastries covered with butter and cinnamon sugar or jam. Sarah, Jan and I come back to our staked-out blue blanket and folding chairs, with our Whales' Tails and banana-strawberry shakes. Sarah watches people over the top of her book, carefully, keeping it to herself. I still can't do Jan's hair right, and we both give it up, but we don't let it bother us.

✻ ✻ ✻

Driving east on the Trans-Canada, having left Birds Hill Park and the Festival early because I have to be at work in Kenora the next morning at 7:00 o'clock, I'm driving straight at a huge sharp-edged wind-sculpted storm cloud, but it's blowing away from me. The highway is soaked, and the grass and shrubs are gleaming green from the rain that's now moving on ahead, with not a drop on me. I'm to pick up "Manitoba corn" for the next day's working retreat, and when I pull into the roadside fruit stand near Prawda the place is a mess. The rain and wind have knocked over the fruit stand awnings, soaked the people and the fruit and the boxes, left puddles large enough to drop into and lose your Nissan King Cab, and the corn is all from Illinois.

I buy some very wet cobs, debating with myself whether to pretend they're from somewhere near Winkler, and then ease out around the puddles toward Kenora. The day and the road feel right.

＊ ＊ ＊

As I amble my truck through the rock cuts between West Hawk Lake and Kenora, with the end-of-day summer sun going down gold and bright over my shoulder, I try to figure out what is so central and sustaining about the Winnipeg Folk Festival. It's probably obvious, yet another example of perception equalling reality, even when unreal. These are four days of the best of hippiedom for all ages, good music, obligatory weirdness or at least extreme relaxation, fine fast food, and the sharing of all of it with friends and friendly strangers. Many times, strangers will nod a smile as you walk by or, in a lineup for a toilet, will talk about a recent set on a nearby stage. Even in the rain, or in front of the Main Stage, crowded and thick with competing stimuli, or in the profit-driven Home Made Village, there is a sense that this is how things should be. A difference, one of them, from thirty years ago, is that everyone here probably knows that things *aren't* like this, not really then and certainly not now. But for four days they are, sort of, with some considerable effort and posing and pretence all that's required to shift this Birds Hill Park island into our mainstream.

Every year there are moments of recall that come, later, to fit the Festival, as there always are with every other year and place and event, some important and some not. Whenever I put on my long-sleeved, blue, round-necked, cotton shirt in the next fall and winter, I'll think of the brief but eye-to-eye conversation with the woman who designed and made it. She had driven her station wagon out from central Ontario, with kids, and looked hot and tired and happy as she accepted praise and money in her Home Made Village stall. The name of her company, her line of clothes, is "Mom Can't Cook." I think of her and her kids and the Under-the-Canvas pan-flute workshop which was going on near her staff as we talked, every time I put on this shirt with the three salamanders on the front. It fits.

As I was leaving the Park grounds that afternoon, strolling to my truck, I passed a mother talking to her son. They were also walking slowly, comfortable with each other, holding hands. He was about five, maybe four, and as I walked past, he looked up at his mother and said, "I'm not leaving here forever." Me too.

Greyhound Fashion
Consultant

Bus #877, non-smoking, non-Express out of Winnipeg, takes Highway #1, the Trans-Canada route. It says CALGARY in large letters, right up front, but I'm only going to Regina.

A skinny, middle-aged man stands at the bus door talking to a large, older woman, who is using a cane. He is inside and she is outside. Her hair is very orange and very thin. He is telling her of the amenities on the bus, listing the toilet, TV and air conditioning. She says that the bus has everything for him, "except for coffee."

The man is wearing black loafers, brown socks, red and blue jogging shorts, and a V-neck T-shirt, white with blue trim. His legs, arms, skin, and eyes have wires just under the surface, hard and tight and jumping. My daughter Sarah would refuse to let me outdoors in his outfit unless she saw it as an anarchistic statement, some sort of mysterious 55-year-old punk/glam equivalent.

We go out Portage Avenue, driving west. A large motorcycle cuts in front of us to save a nanosecond and comes ever so close to being hit. The bus driver, crew cut, with gold-rimmed sunglasses, an aging middleweight, (as are many of us), says, "I didn't see him," and honks some pointed Greyhound scorn down the biker's neck at the next light. The biker doesn't look back, not even a glance.

We fake a stop, a rolling flick of a pause, at all railroad tracks, but we don't hesitate for Weigh Stations. We're on the road, prairie to the left and prairie to the right and a long line of open road ahead to the horizon. We will stop in Brandon in three hours, Regina in eight, and for those with a serious movement addiction, it's on to Calgary in twenty hours. I am just this type of junkie, but am cutting back, even so far as to seek out moments of stillness, very occasionally, but not today.

We pass many cars, as this thing hums right along. It has soft seats, no rattles, tinted glass, and cool air, a long distance from the Acadia Lines buses I used to use in Atlantic Canada, 30 years ago. My last such Atlantic trip was from St. John's to Port Aux Basques, in 1977, when a friend put me on the bus and I got off alone, free as a hitchhiking bird, lonely and happy.

Today, I paid $1.07 extra for the "Seat Selection" option and so have the front seat, window, across the aisle from the driver. We're both quiet types, though, so there's no cross-aisle master-of-the-road chatter.

* * *

Bugs shatter on the windshield. Some of their lives turn into vivid orange Rorschachs; others become clear collages of spiney bits, while an occasional one leaves behind an opaque smudge with a touch of pink at the centre. The bus doesn't seem to have windshield washing equipment, or perhaps Greyhound prefers to pay a small tribute to their insect cousins, leaving the remains to be viewed for a few hours, an open-casket type of arrangement. The birds stay clear of us, with some difficulty in a couple of near-miss cases, and I begin to suspect that a BUS ALERT should be broadcast, if we only knew the language and if we only cared a damn.

✳ ✳ ✳

Near Elie, a person on a tractor is mowing the ditch. She glances at us, then looks back at the ditch.

We cross bridges, over the Assiniboine and the La Salle rivers.

My favourite view on the prairie is that of a farm, a "homestead," carefully surrounded by trees and then fields and nearby buildings and machinery, or so it appears from a distance, looking down the straight dirt road, which leads off from the equally straight, paved highway. There is a self-sufficiency to the image that is appealing, and I study these views but not from up close. Self-sufficiency, like serenity, doesn't bear up well under close observation.

I said that the tree-cloaked farm was my favourite view, out here away from the ocean, but I accidentally lied, a recurring problem. It is in the Top Ten, but the current leader is a train on the very horizon, at dusk just before semi-purple light, straight as a ruled line running east or west; it doesn't matter. Other current contenders for the top spot, edging up on that east-west train, are an early morning at Manitoba's Norris Lake with ducks and mist on the water, or the fall fields of stubble burning as you come down the road from Jackhead to Peguis, the light most perfect at dusk, or a single-engine Otter circling to land on the Burntwood River at Thompson, or the nearby spring flood at Pishew Falls, whose name means the hissing sound of a lynx, in Cree.

✳ ✳ ✳

The bus stops in Portage la Prairie. I've spent a few days in this town, but my feeling of comfort comes more from the fact that I'm from here, figuratively speaking. Kentville, Nova Scotia, and Portage, Manitoba, are identical twins separated at birth. The streets and stores, attitudes and problems, winter jobs and summer grass, all feel like home. We pull into the bus stop, exchange bags and people for new ones, let the smokers get their fix, and move off again onto Highway #1.

✳ ✳ ✳

At the intersection of Highway #1 with the road to Neepawa, the bus stops for the light. A large BEAVER LUMBER truck is parked on the shoulder, and immediately behind it are two hitchhikers—a man and a woman. He is wearing shorts and sneakers and an Australian one-side-up hat, with no shirt to cover a large round abdomen. She has on shorts and shoes and a yellow top, and her stance is the classic hip-tilted, right leg held straight and out a bit, that is so tempting to call gender-specific but is in fact learned, as is the bus driver's way of eating sunflower seeds from a huge bag propped against the windshield. He eats them shells and all. The nature/nurture discussion is *so* long-winded.

The hitchhikers will never get a ride in that position, but maybe they don't care to ride today.

At the Austin Bus Stop and Petro Canada Station, a man is putting gas in his Studebaker President. The car is not as old as I am, but we know each other; we were brought up together.

We stop at Brandon for supper, only 35 minutes to eat and the bus has a "no waiting" policy.

＊ ＊ ＊

Greyhound must already have a fashion consultant, a discreet type, because after Brandon the skinny man is re-dressed in brown pants and a yellow shirt. At a pit stop in Virden, he bums a cigarette from a large man who is wear-ing baggy shorts and a FLORIDA T-shirt, bright pink and lime green on black. A fashion consultant's work is never done.

We get a new driver at Virden. He puts his name in the "Your Driver Is ..." slot, which previously was left empty.

A ground squirrel tries to dart across the road ahead of us, in traffic, and has a large burgundy family-car miss it by centimetres with both front and rear tires. The squirrel goes fast into the ditch, untouched and probably oblivious of the depth of blackness in the shadow that just passed overhead—one spared rodent. God has a challenging sense of humour.

Our new driver, who dares to share his name, has some different twists. He drives more slowly, and a couple of daredevil cars actually pass us, an unheard of event for Bus #877. He's 15 or 20 years older than the first driver, with the balding and paunch and grey all in more advanced stages. The obligatory rudeness is there though, and a woman getting off in Elkhorn, who says a polite and friendly "Thank you very much," doesn't even get a nod. However, lest we think a heart doesn't beat warm and caring in this driver's chest, he does a left-handed wave-salute to each and every large truck we meet. This is a spread-fingered wave, regal and benevolent, index finger elevated, with the rest of the hand fanning out more or less vertically. Not a truck gets missed, and if he's in the middle of shifting gears or inspecting the cargo list, some rapid hand-envelope-gearshift coordination is necessary. Most of the other drivers wave back, and sometimes they wave first.

We enter Saskatchewan without significant applause. I was hoping to focus on the turnoff to St. Lazare but missed it, something I've been doing for years.

* * *

I find the prairie most overwhelming at dusk, when the vastness seems to find a higher level, to simply relax with its size and unfold. It is at this time of day that it seems most closely related to the ocean and the mountains. I suspect that, if I ever achieve maturity, I'll see the same depth in the single leaf of a worm-bitten poplar, but for now I'll take the Winnipeg-Calgary bus, at 9:30 pm, near Grenfell, Saskatchewan, with on-again/off-again rain coming from the layers of black and purple and translucent sunset clouds, and with a freight train meeting us as it goes east, hooting its meaning-of-life choir of a song as it passes about 100 feet off our right hands. Neither the bus driver nor I wave. We don't have to; it's all understood.

* * *

We pull into Indian Head for five minutes, and eight smokers leap out. Nicotine deprivation enhances agility. A cat walks up the ramp of the nearby grain elevator, which is on a tilt of at least 10 degrees. The cat pauses to look around, then walks off and down the other side out of sight, into cat history. I wonder if the residents of Indian Head consider their town's name to be racist, reducing scores of nations to the stereotypic sameness of "Indian." A round town sign sports an "Indian" male in traditional headgear. Do the Chicago Blackhawks and the Cleveland Indians and the Atlanta Braves struggle on a regular basis, say at semi-annual hymn sings, with their teams' willingness to use oppressed nations as mascots? But then (hold on just a damn minute now) what about the Montreal Canadiens, and the New York Yankees, and the Mariners, and Whalers, and Astros? I search the memory banks for Caucasian and dominant-culture town names. About a half hour later, as we near Regina, I do a mental genuflection to the Great Ironist, as we pass a turn-off sign to White City.

✻ ✻ ✻

I pause in Regina.

✻ ✻ ✻

Two days later, Bus #737, non-smoking Express to Winnipeg en route to Toronto, leaves at 8:15 am. This bus only stops at Whitewood, Virden and Brandon before getting to Winnipeg in 560 km and 7½ hours.

I don't get the front seat across the aisle from the driver, as a fifteen-year-old beats me to it. He's wearing jeans, sneakers, a white T-shirt, and a Foster's Lager ball cap—the complete uniform and very well put together, a fashion consultant's dream. He's also got a skull and cross-bones earring, left ear, and expensive-looking headphones. I've been replaced by a rookie and a trendy one at that. I

nurse a wounded-ego sulk as we aim dead east, past road
signs to Pilot Butte, Buffalo Lookout, Fort Qu'Appelle,
Yorkton, and Weyburn.

✳ ✳ ✳

Saskatchewan is green, and I hope that it is more than a
surface cosmetic hiding a drought lurking just inches
down, as this province has been very dry the last few years.

We pass many grain elevators, and I marvel at them,
their sore-thumb, clunky grace. They remind me of
Maritime lighthouses with their sentinel attitudes and their
shared origins of responding to necessary outlooks and hard
times as well as the shared present tense of economic and
technological battering. If fog and ships are the lifeblood of
lighthouses, then grain and the urgency of cooperation give
these square-cornered relatives their purpose.

We pass abandoned farmhouses on our left and grain
elevators on our right, as we enter Whitewood, driving
into full prairie morning sun.

The kid who took over my position and got me
reduced to backup starts to talk, and I get a whiff of the
veteran giving the rookie some valuable tips, to be
acknowledged later when he plays in his first All Star
game. This image fades quickly as the rookie does most of
the talking with me playing the nodding listener. He is
from BC, going to Thunder Bay. He left Vancouver yesterday morning and the trip will take two days, costing
$142, "one way, and $10 of that is GST." His family used
to live in Thunder Bay, but they moved west for jobs. He's
in grade 9, "except for math; that's still grade 8," and he
likes the view of the mountains from their BC carport. He

does not like the gangs. He had a gang member cock a rifle and point it at him recently, when he came over a hill on his dirt bike in some back fields and surprised a group standing there with guns, "but he didn't shoot." His family is going to move to another town, where there aren't so many gangs.

One of the reasons for his visit to Thunder Bay is so he can visit the local "cop shop." There is an ongoing misunderstanding about payment of fines for his driving a dirt bike recklessly, without insurance and without a license. He says that his mother paid the fines, but the police say she didn't. He sold the bike to a friend and is looking forward to getting back on it.

He knows a guy in Winnipeg and asks if I know him. I don't.

✳ ✳ ✳

We stop in Virden and then in Brandon for lunch. Soon after leaving Brandon, we pass several hitchhikers. They don't seem to know what they're doing, standing in places where cars will find it difficult to stop, or smoking, or lying on the ground, a position which has not been politically correct since 1966 but didn't lead to many rides then, either.

There is a rhythm to skilled hitchhiking. You must look very neutral but appropriately needy and potentially grateful, and you've got to be in a place where the car can let you in with ease. Gently and safely rejecting offers from drunks and overt whackos is an art, as is passing on the offer from the kindly person who's only going 12 miles down the road and will then let you out on the longest stretch of godforsaken wind-blown high-speed highway you've ever seen in your life. Signs announcing where you're going will help and so do clean clothes. A beard does not help, and a cigarette cuts off a growing sane segment of the population. If you can get in with a trucker, say at the exit to a truck stop, then life suddenly looks very fine. I've gone with truckers from St. Anthony to Gander in Newfoundland, from Bangor, Maine, to Boston, and many times from Sackville, New Brunswick, to Kentville, Nova Scotia, and the ride was always high, fast and serious, which puts it right up there beside baseball in the Allegory-For-a-Lifetime category.

Hitching rides with planes, helicopters, and freighter ships in Labrador and the NWT was also an acquired skill, with a higher degree of difficulty in some ways, but also more dependence on basic grovelling combined with lies. I keep waiting for the local universities, when they finally switch to a progressive mode, to ask me to do a course called "Hitchhiking 201—Highways and Flyways." The prerequisite would be 5,000 miles of land-based hitching or 50,000 miles in the air. Water travel would be a non-credit elective, as it would unfairly discriminate against Alberta and Saskatchewan, the only provinces or territories not blessed with salt water. Fresh-water freeloading won't count a damn. (My other course will be "Biases 801," and it would have a *lot* of prerequisites.)

✿ ✿ ✿

I sleep most of the way from Portage to Winnipeg. We arrive five minutes early, and I go looking for a Winnipeg Transit ride home.

You're either on the bus or off the bus, or so we've all been told, and it appears that I am on. My only problem is that I'm not dressed appropriately for the city bus ride home.

Adjudicating Fragments

One of the most startlingly influential books of my life had the approximate title of notes-from-a-bottle-found-on-the-beach-at-Carmel, but I forget the author's name and the exact title. I came on it in my early 20s, and it was a bright flash, revealing fragments of life and thought, and challenging the reader to connect things, if you dared. The idea of life as fragments requiring the effort of connection is a sustaining one, taking away some of the sad edge of Paul Simon's warning that ". . . everything put together falls apart . . . ," instead making it simply a necessity to see the new evolving connections.

For example, as a younger adult I used to see the falling down houses and barns in grown-over Nova Scotian and Labrador yards as painfully sad, dormer windows on sag, front door open to rain and squirrel, lives and hopes and promises having been lived there, spent there.

I feel the sight from another angle now. That land sustained those people in that time when it and they could, and the house is now going to change to poplar and alder, tall grass and low berries, a true recycle. Everything put together falls apart, and then comes together again, differently. My own collection of images, for now, would be "Fragments from a truck somewhere south of Sioux Lookout," but I have to make the connection.

✳ ✳ ✳

I take some days off to watch my kids dance in a Festival. They are amazing to watch, aware of their abilities but unsure of their potential, struggling to find the heart of the dance and of themselves. The adjudicators, like any judges or critics I've ever known, are dazzling in their shift between love of the topic and ego-based posturing, and also between gentle caring and brutal judgments. I would dearly love to hear more about the aim and ability of dance to assist our lives through body awareness, joy of movement, and self-control, and the essential connection between body and ground, but this only rarely and tangentially gets mentioned. Instead, most of the judging chatter is about where arms and legs should and should not be held, about distribution of weight and being "back off the centre," and sadly about whether the dance achieved "gold" or "silver" or "bronze." The unrealistic jubilation of those who "got a gold" and unrealistic devastation of those who "only got a bronze" is wrong to watch, but in the land of coloured credit cards and election-night counts, how can we expect anything less? The judges and the dancers are of our society and have little choice.

I watch my kids and their friends in a huge production number, *The Lion King*, and am again reassured by their ability to camp it up and soar with lethal hyena grace and to genuinely laugh and share affection, all in the midst of people intent on judging them, both groups apparently oblivious to the risk of undermining connections.

One of the dance adjudicators is severe in her marking, but is consistently kind in her comments, especially in her use of tone of voice and direct eyes and humour. I watch her, not only when she is on stage at the microphone, herself performing in front of the dancers and audience, but also when she is sitting at the long adjudication table. The table is centre theatre, with a couple of small dim goose-necked lights. There is a stage director with a headset coordinating, I assume, music and entrances and lights, then the adjudicator in the centre, and to her right an assistant who prepares the certificates for each dancer. This particular centered adjudicator rests her cropped head on her hands and just lets her eyes go to the music, the dance and, possibly, when she can, to the connections. Even though like most specialists she sometimes misses the forest for the trees, she is saved by her heart and so, therefore, are the dancers. My judgment of her adjudication is favourable, but I refuse on principle to award a gold or bronze or silver.

✳ ✳ ✳

As with most people who write words in a row, I send them to people for consideration for publication or, as we so aptly put it in this society, I "submit" them. The process of submission is, for some, a particularly irksome one, but what's a scribbler, or a dancer, to do?

Those on the receiving end of submissions are revealing and influential in their responses. When I was starting to write fiction, for example, I would regularly send in short pieces to *The New Yorker*, mostly just for the rush of putting the short story in an envelope addressed to that brilliant magazine and then having the courage and arrogance to actually mail it. The rejection slips were themselves classic New Yorker pieces, typed small cards with an artistic flair but impersonal. They left neither disappointment nor anger, just a cool chill. Somewhere in the middle of the rejection spectrum was a note from an eastern publisher, hand-typed and loaded with typos and grammatical blunders, insensitive to an Olympian level in its dissection of my work, and ending with the macho admonition, ". . . tough, but there it is." I corrected his note with red ink in a world-weary English 100 professional tone, grading it a D, and mailed it back to him. We don't exchange birthday cards.

The most wonderful rejection slip of my life came from Robert Weaver, when he was editing an annual Canadian anthology of short fiction. I submitted a story, which I still think was pretty good, and has since been published. His rejection note was handwritten, personal and kind, gently and even shyly pointing out some flaws in pacing and characterization that were useful and wise and not at all discouraging. Quite the opposite, because as I read this rejection slip, I felt that I was being spoken to as a writer, a wonderful gift.

In the randomly brilliant and always whimsical television series *Northern Exposure*, Ed Chigliak episodically struggles with his own personal demon, that of self-doubt leading to the need for "external validation." It is implied that the alternative, the need for internal validation, is more just and less superficial, but I'm not so sure. You pay your time, and your demons pick you, and they're all a pain, all the validators. We need more Robert Weavers, externally and internally, to craft our adjudications and successes and rejections into fulfilling moments of growth. We do live in hope, every day.

Maugham's Room

Bangkok is an assault. The heat, traffic, noise, pollution, crowds, vendors, humidity, choices, rain, and tourists are all overwhelming and out of control. I spend several days in and out of Bangkok, wandering and being led for two days each in Sukolnakhor and Sukothai provinces, in the northeast and northwest, but always coming back to Bangkok. My role is that of a two-week consultant-in-public-health on a mostly symbolic and ceremonial inspection-of-grant-recipients tour. I'm a paid tourist. This is my first trip to Asia, and I end up bringing back gifts and a report and significant culture shock, but mostly I bring cakes and ale, snapshots taken on all sides while overwhelmed. I don't use a camera.

✳ ✳ ✳

At 6:00 am, I go for a jog, having been told by a host about an appropriate park nearby. I partly go for the exertion of it but also partly to give my day some sense of normality, my usual ritual transplanted from the Winnipeg "Y" or the

101

city streets, a transparent and somewhat pathetic cultural-protection ruse, but if it works, what the hell.

The park is busy at 6:00 am; hundreds of kids playing soccer, street sweepers, Thai joggers, people sleeping on benches, vendors setting up food stalls, people just out for a stroll, and this one middle-aged North American jogger sweating along in faded Adidas shorts and sneakers and a grey "Dalvey By The Sea, PEI" T-shirt. The temperature is already at 30 degrees Celsius. I do two laps and give it up, going back to the hotel to get ready for the day of meetings.

✻ ✻ ✻

As I walk back, I think over the dry facts I've read before coming here. They are true but they are not enough; they don't capture the impact of the city. Bangkok has about six million people, the books said, but the number doesn't begin to tell of the heavy pressing proximity of so many, of the people sleeping in doorways or begging gently but definitely to your face. It misses the sidewalks thick with people eating at tables and selling from stalls and walking so casually, and most especially it misses the simple unrelenting push on the senses.

In Thai the name for Bangkok is Krung Thep, meaning heavenly city or city of angels. Maybe and maybe not because, if they're out there, they fly right on by me, with not a nudge.

When I was in high school in Nova Scotia, I had an English teacher who felt I had the capability of doing more than vainly attempting to be a jock, skipping school, and ingratiating myself with other jocks and pseudo-jocks. I've always felt that Mr. Carter had a severely limited definition of excellence and that he failed to recognize my considerable layabout and treading-water abilities. These abilities continue to sustain me.

Mr. Carter persuaded me to read *Cakes and Ale* by Somerset Maugham, for a book-report exercise. My usual ploy was to read about ten scattered pages of a book, always including the first and last pages, and then write a general vague state-of-the-world report that could *not* be failed; guaranteed. It also couldn't get over a C- grade, but (as the Labradorians say) "What odds?" On this particular occasion, Mr. Carter really turned up the heat, virtually coercing me into actually reading the book. I *loved* it and quickly read everything of Maugham's I could find. (Mr. Carter hid his gloating remarkably well.) Somewhere in Maugham's work, and I haven't the faintest memory where, he refers to Bangkok's Oriental Hotel, with respect and affection bordering on genuflection, or at least that's how I remember it from grade 10.

I go for lunch at the Oriental twice, once with a colleague and once on my own. The *Verandah* restaurant sits beside the Chao Phraya River, Thailand's main river and the one that makes Bangkok a major port. This wide and crowded river highway begins as many separate streams in the northern mountains, combining to form rivers in the central plain of the country, which lies between the mountains' foothills and the Gulf of Thailand. Four of these rivers, the Nan, Ping, Wang, and Yom, come together on the plain to become the Chao Phraya. The largest part of Bangkok sits on the east bank of the river, about 25 kilometres from the gulf. I read that the river used to dominate the city, but now the tide has turned, the canals are being filled in, and the city is in charge, for a while.

I wander around the Oriental, trying to see if it has formed a significant truce with Chao Phraya, if it fits. The hotel is expensive, with signs implying that if they don't like the cut of your clothes, you're history. There are platoons of workers vacuuming thick rugs that were last vacuumed eighteen minutes ago, and polishing brass handrails, and scrutinizing passersby to weed out any interloping scum. I'm ready for them, socks on, hair combed, a nonchalant and confident attitude, and a shopping bag in hand from a well-known expensive store I visited two days before. We Nova Scotians can fake out an elitist from twenty paces away, any day. (It's when they come up close that we have problems.)

After wandering the halls and shops, searching for Maugham's ghost, who is evidently long gone, I settle in for a beer-soaked lunch, about thirty feet from the river. Lunch is standard rich people's fare, not worth mentioning, but the river is magnificent. There are thousands of floating plants, hyacinths I'm told, and almost as many boats. My favourites are long, flat-bottomed and narrow, with a huge motor at the back which makes them fly. They do not bother with mufflers, at least not at an auditory glance. The motor has a long rudder-like appendage jutting back into the water, with a propeller on the end. I can see the tourists' heads snap back as buddy guns it. The river laughs.

Also on the river are shuttle boats going from hotel to hotel, both large and small ferries, and barges of high, wide and thick, black-bottomed bulk, pulled by the long, narrow hot-rods. One large, old, wood-hulled boat goes by, my favourite for the day. It is shaped somewhat like a junk but with no sails, and it has a wide, thick rudder and cargo piled on deck. It moves with a slow, heavy grace. Maugham might have liked that boat, as he viewed it from the Oriental Verandah, sipping ale.

✳ ✳ ✳

We visit twelve villages in northern Thailand in two days. The other Canadian I'm travelling with is excellent in cross-cultural village situations, and I'm not so shabby either, if given a chance, but we don't get much of a chance. This is the visiting-dignitaries type of jaunt, complete with ten-minute stops per village, greeting speeches here and there, and the general feeling of the two sides peering over a fence at each other. Even so, it's difficult to be denied a glimpse. Thai houses in the villages are built with two stories, living quarters upstairs, often partially open, and an exposed under-area for storage and hammocks and playing children and animals. Shoes are not worn upstairs. Water is collected from roofs into large water jars. Everyone I see wears rubber thongs or open-heeled sandals.

Several mothers are rocking babies in makeshift hammocks, much like those I have seen in Davis Inlet, Labrador, or Little Grand Rapids, Manitoba. One of the hosts has visited Peguis Reserve in Manitoba, and he smiles when I tell him of these hammocks. I remember his visit, about a year before, as I had set it up and accompanied him on parts of the trip. When meeting the Chief of one Reserve we visited, I was struck, as I lurked at the edges and watched, by how he and his companion, both people of colour, were accepted with warmth and a sense of shared history and entitlement and turmoil. I am way too white for my own good, and for anyone else's good as well.

The Thai villages are like home to me, and I feel grounded, comfortable and relaxed as we walk around, stay in small hotels, eat in village restaurants, and talk in places where we stand around like real people, with faces smiling real smiles. I'm glad to have seen Bangkok and hope I never go there again. This is where I'll stay, in my head.

There are moments that impinge on me in a way that will make them last, scenes that will recur, frequently for no recognized reason, probably a sound or a smell, a spoken phrase or a mannerism. Somebody recently told me, as they walked away, that "life is a memory." I agree. There is no present, no future, just stories and retained images and, if we are lucky and skillful, connections.

These moments take varying shapes. In one town we stop our van to watch rowers practice on the river for the races to be held during an upcoming holiday. We have a privileged view in the almost-empty seating area, facing the river, watching a casual practice race, graceful effort in bright sun, with the long boats gliding by.

In many towns I am taken to see Buddhist temples. I've apparently made my interest plain, perhaps in ways I haven't realized. In one temple, our older and more solemn guide tells me to sit quietly and, with head empty of thoughts, concentrate on the Buddha. This Buddha is reclining, on his side, and the space in front of him does generate a sense of calm, even though people are moving in and out all the time. I sit for a while and then my host comes to get me, saying we have to go. He doesn't ask or tell me anything. I will try this.

We also see many water buffalo and people working in fields of water, and I learn a bit about holy trees. My attempts to find vegetarian meals are suddenly made easier, when I accidentally discover that it is just at the end of "Chinese Lent." When I use that phrase, people look at my big-nosed, round-eyed Caucasian state with a quizzical eyebrow lift, but then easily give over the vegetables, no meat, no problem.

As the days go by, I'm finding the food easier, the humidity less draining, and my internal comfort level stabilizing. The sidewalk stalls have some wonderful bargains mixed in with the rip-offs, and I buy gifts and many bootlegged cassettes at one dollar a pop. I even learn to do the form of respectful salutation that combines hands folded in front of chest with a slight bent-forward head-tilt. This brings huge grins to several Thai faces.

✳ ✳ ✳

One of the hosts has told me that Thailand is the only country in this entire region not to have been occupied by Europeans and that the country's anthem is "land of the free." Coming from North America, that is a phrase I've heard before, both in celebration and in tragic irony. In Thailand, however, I have a sense of the compromise and effort that has made the theme true. As I get on the Bangkok plane to go to Hong Kong, then Vancouver, then Winnipeg, I nod to this desperate city of free angels. I may come back, after all.

A Welcome Dread

I live, for now, in Kenora, Ontario, and am on my way to a medical conference in Vancouver. I've decided to try for the short-term great escape by stitching several holiday days onto my study leave. On the drive into Winnipeg, I visualize the trip route, while listening to Joe Cocker over and over, cranked, trying to catch his subtle nuances, certain they exist. He speaks of "many rivers to cross" and of the need to find his way over, sounding aware of other times when rivers were obstacles and most people weren't lost.

My route is planned to include a drive to Winnipeg, flight to Edmonton, bus to Prince Rupert, ferry to Port Hardy, bus to Nanaimo, ferry to Vancouver, flight to Winnipeg, and then the drive back home to Kenora in an increasingly shaky and travel-weary light pickup truck. I am sure there will be a few rivers along the way and wonder if I'm up to crossing if the bridges are out.

✳ ✳ ✳

The wall of one of my rooms at home has a map of Canada with previously travelled roads marked off, first in yellow, then topped in blue. The result is as it should be, a maze without a centre. The map itself is another story, stolen from a book I gave a person who was then a friend but now is not. When I think of this person, or the others who once were close and came to be nothing but a sad or warm memory, I occasionally remember Neil Young's words, *". . . thinking about what a friend had said; hoping it was a lie."* Don't we all.

✳ ✳ ✳

Before leaving Kenora, I picked up my mail and found a letter from a friend I hadn't heard from in months. While waiting in the Winnipeg airport, I open it, carefully, slowly, noting the absence of return address and the reversion to "Peter" in my name.

Most friends call me "Pete," my used name, my pre-medicine name. What we call people seems to take on a rigid quality, separate from the shifting reality of the person they're trying to be; the names are fixed. Kay or Cathie to Kate, friend to stranger, Anthony to Tony, partner to enemy, Emmy to Emily, Ingy to Katherine, Pete to Peter and back again; who could keep up? Who would want to, when it's so much easier just to sign into the concrete gallery? This is the way it was when I knew you, and this is the way I'm keeping it, keeping you.

My friend is still my friend; as the letter is affectionate, generous and without demands. I've been worrying for nothing, inventing alienations. How many times does this happen? Then again, how many times is affection invented as well? This river flows both ways at once, and I wonder what to call it. Perhaps I'll just swim in it, naked of course, and let the ambivalent thief name itself.

✵ ✵ ✵

We cross the North Saskatchewan River as we drive into Edmonton, from the airport at Nisqu. The Winnipeg-to-Edmonton flight was a classic exercise in travel plans shagged-up, gone awry, seeking and sustaining a cumulative negative roll. The connecting flight from Hamilton to Winnipeg, we were told as we sat late and glum in the departure area, ran into a storm in the sky, complete with upheaval of people and coffee and stomachs, so they turned tail and went back. Their problem becomes our problem, as they own the plane until it gets to Winnipeg. We sit and read and walk around and wait. They get in two hours late, so we arrive in Edmonton three hours late, and many of us miss our buses and planes and appointments and friends. People are not amused in the 1:00 am shuttle van crossing the North Saskatchewan.

The Winnipeg airline people had reluctantly admitted that they were responsible for our hotel in Edmonton and that we should arrange this at the Edmonton airport counter. In Edmonton, the counter is closed. The rolling scoreboard records AIRLINES SIXTY ZILLION AND ONE, PASSENGERS ZIP, and the shuttle bus drops several of us at the downtown hotel sidewalk with a quite warm "good luck."

One of the shuttle drop-offs is a Canadian Military Reserves trainee, going home to visit Jasper before being posted at Edmonton. We have missed the same bus. After the gathering of luggage and multiple muttering departures into the quiet Edmonton night, she and I are the only two left on the sidewalk. "I don't know where I'm going to stay; haven't got much money," she says in a low voice, more to herself than to me.

I pause, not wanting to be here, in this. But I am, so I say, "If you think you'd be comfortable sharing a room with a stranger, non-smoking, two beds, you're welcome to stay with me." She is comfortable, and she does stay. As we spend the late night and then the early morning sharing a bedroom and bathroom, we manage. We talk, in the light and in the dark, and we relax, and even approach friendliness. But we do not connect, not really, and I wonder again what it is that allows some people just to *see* each other and is missing from so many others, from most of us.

She leaves at 6:00 am, running for her bus and thanking me for the room. I say "you're welcome," and mean it, then roll over and go back to sleep.

✻ ✻ ✻

On the Edmonton to Prince Rupert bus, we stop at several places for passengers, freight, food, smokes, bathrooms, the whole spectrum. Two people from England are in Canada for their first visit, on their way to the mountains. They are older than I am. He says, "You have to do this while you can." I agree, adding, "All of us do," but he doesn't bite. I sit, watching the road, and remember a woman I was watching at the Edmonton airport, from inside the parked shuttle van while it was waiting to fill. The woman was tall, dressed in an elegant long burgundy skirt with a well-cut dark green jacket and black high-heeled shoes. She was waiting just in front of the curb, not smoking or appearing to be watching, just waiting. After a few minutes she took her right foot out of the high-heeled shoe, slowly flexed it up and down, back and forth, then did the same with the left foot, relaxing from the damn shoes while she could.

✳ ✳ ✳

Riding on the bus is sometimes like following behind a serious and unyielding flat earth snake, watching it unfold. At other times, it's a series of one-liners, some funny and some sad. The distinctions are not always easy to make. Today, between Jasper and Prince Rupert:

- two people share the view from the bus with sensitivity and humour, and with apparent respect for each other, as they don't intrude on silences or interrupt speech. They sometimes just point out something, a bridge or an angled tree or a fine house, and it is acknowledged with a nod or smile, and twice with a touch of a knee. They like each other;

- scatter my ashes in amongst the spruce; the more scraggly the better, preferably on some rock perch near the water, with a high and wide view, out of reach of the loggers but with threats of avalanche or budworm or wildfire at my back to keep me honest;

- the Skeena river starts off narrow and shallow, or so it looks from seat A2 on bus #925, but it soon becomes wide and fast. I soon realize that I have absolutely no idea what this or any other river is about: origins, routes, inhabitants and neighbours, destinations, threats and strengths; you name it, and I don't know it. In spite of that, the many people fishing off the sandbars and rock bars of the Skeena do appear to be enjoying themselves; fishing for sockeye, the driver tells me;

- a child at the back of the bus has to say "daddy, daddy, daddy" over and over before he gets answered, usually seven to ten times, with rising volume. This is apparently old news to both father and son, as neither seems to notice;

- I have never been on this road in my life and am elated at the deep strange newness of it;

- the "rock cuts," those slashes through huge stands of stone to allow the highway passage, are similar to north-western Ontario's Shield, except these have moss growing on the rocks, green and thick. This is flat-out not allowed where I'm from;

- we have murdered hundreds of bugs with our windshield as we cruise the snaking ribbon. At our stop in Valemont, I get the windshield cleaner implement from the Petro Canada pumps and reach as high as I can. The driver asks if I want to drive as well, but later tells me it does look bet-ter and maybe he should occasionally do this himself. No criticism implied, I tell him—just doing my part.

※ ※ ※

Prince Rupert is like mixing St. John's, with its gulls and hills, land-stacked harbours and working boats and its ordinary small buildings, in with Kenora's affluence and smaller size, float planes and fleet of recreational boats. I go on like this, in my head, as I wander the streets. The city is hugely attractive (of course, I've hit a sunny day, one of the eight this fall, I'm told) and definitely marine. It is also at the end of the road, a blessing as far as I'm concerned, but opinions on that seem to vary. Not mine, as I plead for the fates to give me a year or three here, sometime, later.

✳ ✳ ✳

There are flowers in Prince Rupert, on houses and walks, at public buildings, some growing wild but mostly not; they're everywhere. The scent is even in the air, again and again, occasionally thick and sweet and close, but more often just a whiff, subtle and welcome. In partnership with the flowers is the massive looming green of the surroundings, dripping even when not raining, moving toward any open space, a pushing growth with no need of help. I remember a CBC interview with someone on a Gulf Island who was coming close to complaining about the invasion of plants, of the need to keep them in check or become overgrown. What a way to go, to be overcome by cedar and spruce and flower and moss, a slow merging partnership of a death.

✳ ✳ ✳

After breakfast at Cow Bay, just off from central Prince Rupert, a routine post-muffin making-conversation question results in some wonderful future trip information. I am the advance guard, and friend Ben will be pleased to hear of the Skeena railway option from Edmonton to Prince Rupert, with an overnight in Prince George. My occasional enthusiasm for marathon bus trips is not shared by most humans and the train will probably appeal more. I'm also told of a route to Skagway, Alaska, by taking a float plane to Ketchikan and then the regular ferry on up the coast. I have also seen an ad for legal hitchhiking on a mail plane run out of Ketchikan, so future trips are taking shape. The one flickering in today's future-tense includes taking the ferry from Port Hardy to Prince Rupert, to stay at the Eagle Bluff Bed and Breakfast, then several days on the Queen

Charlotte Islands and back to Prince Rupert, and fly to Ketchikan and explore there for a couple of days, then on ferry to Skagway, and finally find a way to Whitehorse.

There it loses focus. The return trip is always the hardest part to plan, whether to circle or backtrack, take half the time and just flash on home, or whether to return at all—the recurring question.

✳ ✳ ✳

The Queen of the North ferry goes from Prince Rupert to Port Hardy in 15 hours, with only about two hours of mild, hold-on-to-your-stomach swells. We see hill upon steep-wooded hill folded in on each other, some with rock faces where even the spruce can't cling and a few with waterfalls that are more like water slides, as the thin stream falls straight and white, tight against the rock, a tentative lasting relationship.

We go through multiple showers, leaving rainbows in fragments behind us as we pass tugboats pulling barges loaded with timber and long-liners going toward where they hope the fish are, or back from the same place.

We also go by several lighthouses. A few months ago, on a whim after hearing some CBC interview, I called Ottawa and British Columbia to find out about the possibility of working at a lighthouse. They said I would definitely qualify, if only it was twenty years ago. They're going to automate the whole chain of lighthouses, within three years, all of them. I'll have to work on my timing.

One of the lighthouses we pass is particularly wonderful, on an island with the house tucked back into some sheltering trees, only a few steps from the flashing-eye office. There is also a walking bridge to the mainland, in case some friend simply has to have a place to walk, away from the building and toward the wolves. I may call again, to see if they'll rethink this whole computer infatuation.

We see some orca near the shore, blowing and breaching. I hope they're playing. The singer in the Dogwood Lounge sings a fine version of Sade's "Smooth Operator," easily keeping time with my Canterbury "dark and mild" beer. Two people across from me play crib without speaking, while at another table, two others rub hands and knees and eyes. I prefer their game; fifteen two, fifteen four, and a pair is six, without the necessity of cards.

I've been looking forward to seeing Bella Bella, but we're going to detour well wide of the town, as the nets are out for "the fall run." We steam on toward the dark and Port Hardy, with high cloud and rain on the windows and on the back. "Some say, love, it is a river," the singer tells us. A man opposite me keeps time on his right knee and mouths the words in unison, gently, no big show. He has a black peaked cap, long, white hair and beard, a green plaid wool vest over a brown corduroy sweatshirt and jeans with black boots. He looks like a grand river himself.

The singer follows up with Van Morrison's "Brown-Eyed Girl," and Whitebeard particularly likes this; it's his age. Me, too; I miss Van so much I could weep, right here in the Dogwood, wondering what happened to the moondance and the slim slow sliding that just faded away. I clap instead and mean every beat of it. The singer takes a break.

✳ ✳ ✳

I listen to two artists discussing painting techniques. They have just met and are sitting at separate tables, in a noisy bar, so my eavesdropping is overt, and they don't care.

One, the more experienced or vocal one, tells the other of a watercolour painter who uses white in his painting, even though you are not supposed to (or at least that's how I hear it; I haven't a clue, but as usual, it doesn't matter). The white-using watercolourist has said "it's *my* painting, and I'll do it any way I want to." Apparently, he sells his work. I know I'll be looking to buy one, should I ever see it, awash in white.

✳ ✳ ✳

The Bed & Breakfast owner in Port Hardy meets me at the door at midnight, barefoot and friendly. He has rented my room but has bounced his son out of his own bed in Room 1, second floor. I crawl in at around 12:30 am, read for a few minutes, and plan to wake up at about 7:00 am, to catch the 8:30 am bus to Nanaimo.

The owner and I have breakfast together in the morning, being bypassed by two very surly and tired-looking people, a woman and a teenaged boy. I thank the boy for the use of his room; no reply. I say "good morning," to the sweat-suited woman; no reply. I ask the man if he minds the constant flow of strangers through his space, explaining that having a Bed & Breakfast is something I have considered doing (a partial truth). (A friend, in a recent note, has offered the opinion that *all* truths are partial, but there are points along that continuum as well.) He grins and says it doesn't bother him much, usually, but I have possibly noticed that his family doesn't like it. I accept more coffee.

We exchange biographies, also partial. He has been a helicopter pilot, including time in the Arctic, so we talk a bit of shared landing places in Coppermine and Yellowknife and of life on the BC coast compared to the

Arctic coast. He is direct and clever, is still in bare feet, and his plans for expansion to a hostel, and for further renovations to the already beautiful house, are fascinating fun and sustaining. I like his coffee and his feet and his ideas. The muffins are burned, but he doesn't apologize for this so I don't have to explain that I prefer them that way. He wouldn't have believed it anyway, even though it is true; partially. I promise to return and mean it; totally.

✳ ✳ ✳

I manage to get the front seat on the bus, across the aisle from the driver. This always requires a certain degree of brazen forwardness and is one of those times a personality defect does get the desired result, but at what eternal cost? The driver is a chatterer, so what the hell; I lean forward, arms on the front-seat railing, and we talk about logging, and Ontario vs. British Columbia weather, the state of the highway, and his prior railway and recreational-vehicle sales work, both of us ignoring the sign that orders DO NOT TALK TO DRIVER WHILE BUS IS IN MOTION. He has absolutely no interest in me, which is just fine, but he's simply talking to pass the time, not as warm or friendly as he appears, I am guessing.

Things go fairly well, in spite of the fact that I would rather watch than talk, which the driver either doesn't notice or doesn't care about. However, at a "fifteen minutes and fifteen minutes only, and I *mean* it" coffee stop, I blow it. I have toast and coffee, line up for the bus-busy washroom, and make the fatal mistake of including the emotional necessity of a phone call, long distance. I'm late for the bus. The driver has, I am told, come close to leaving and will now be running behind schedule, tapping his watch. I get stony looks from the other passengers, all of whom were firmly seated and on time (but back in the cheap seats, I think to myself). I adopt an appropriately sheepish expression, thanking the gods for my Catholic guilt-and-shame-based upbringing, and settle back to see how this plays out, including my own response to social disapproval.

The driver doesn't talk to me anymore, sitting firm-jawed with a faint flush. Didn't take much to wreck that love affair, I think, and not for the first time in my life. I am able to do a lot more tree and hill and water watching as a result of my ostracization, so I cope. It is of some interest to me, though, that I do feel badly, ashamed and stupid even, and am yet again impressed at the extreme power of social approval and disapproval. On this particular day, in this ever-so-forgiving society, I do avoid banishment, by a whisker or two, and after an hour the driver starts to soften and chat again as we approach Campbell River. He cannot stand the silence and so he gives me a break, even advising me to take the later scenic run to Nanaimo instead of the express route. I thank him, feeling my shame wash away but not to be forgotten, not for a while.

※ ※ ※

I have been advised that I should have stayed in Campbell River, or "even Port Hardy," rather than spending two days in Nanaimo, which is characterized as "just another city."

Not quite. I spend a whole day walking the waterfront, in full sun, watching the boats and seagulls and the afflu-ence and apartments. It is a gorgeous place. I've been here before, and it was a gorgeous place then, too.

I can't find a bathroom on the waterfront, so I slip into brazen gear and try to fake my way into a fancy waterside hotel lobby washroom. No luck. Instead, I stumble on an arena, a rink in summer, where the door is open but there's not a person in sight. The interior lights are out, except for a couple, and a rock radio station is blasting away on the high loudspeakers. The ice is in, with lines painted for hockey, and it is shining, unmarked. I find the washroom in the basement, then come back upstairs to stand at the back of the seats for a few minutes, watching the ice. It is perfect.

Two sales people in a "Native Arts and Crafts" store allow me to do a long slow browse, dressed in jogging shorts and sneakers and T-shirt. All three of us know something about the topic, with regional differences. The store is quiet and they are warm generous people, so we spend a pleasant half-hour discussing carving and weaving, woods and whales, aboriginal and sales realities, and by extension, the future of us all. I wish I could invest in their shop, but then again, maybe I have.

There is a long pier that pokes out into the Nanaimo harbour, and I spend a fine sun-soaked hour with my shirt off while watching boats and planes, sitting on the very end of the concrete wharf, legs out over the water. Two women come up beside me, and one laughs, a very pleasant sound, and says she is "*so* tempted to give a little push." She doesn't push, and neither do I.

We talk for a few minutes, and it seems quick and funny and warm. We're having one of those accidental encounters between strangers, where you wish it could last or extend into a book club or supper or offices on the same floor but know it can't and that you will harm the moment if you try for more. They leave, reluctantly it seems, and I watch more boats and water movement, legs still out over the water.

I take a long winding walk home to the hotel, and along the way come on a spit of land sticking out onto the harbour, obviously people-built, with a park bench at the end. This narrow jut of land has a paved path down the middle, and on either side, sloping down to the water, are hundreds of balanced rocks, angled, appearing to be precarious. Some of the structures are small and some are big, some consisting of many rocks and some of fewer, and some include driftwood but most do not. I stop walking, transfixed, and just focus on the intricacy of the balances achieved, not touching or getting too close, just looking. Whoever has done these structures has a pool hustler's sense of angles and a gymnast's sense of balance. They are standing every which way: big on small and the other, round on angular and the other, straight up and off to the sides, just a couple or a whole bunch, near the water and back from it. They all have one thing in common; they've been done with care.

The balances are wonderful, random, whimsical, and they work; they do not come crashing down, not even when scrutinized. I can't help myself, though, and soon start to wonder why? and who? and instead of just enjoying the balanced angles achieved, insist on looking for the angle of motivation. A man comes by with, but separate from, two women, and he reads my face. He tells me that someone from Nanaimo does this—one person, where I had thought it was many or even all of us. He usually has a coffee tin open nearby for appreciative donations. "Does he make a living at it? Good on him if he does; they're great." I have missed him, so don't get to contribute; next time, if we're both lucky.

✳ ✳ ✳

On the Nanaimo-to-Vancouver ferry the next day, soon after we leave, a deeply serious voice comes loudly over the ship's speakers, announcing "Attention Passengers! Hot dogs are *now* available in the Snack Bar." In the crowded eating and observation area, some other hot dog shouts out, "oh, my God! Yes!," getting general laughter in response. The room converges in the shared smiles of strangers.

✹ ✹ ✹

At dinner in Vancouver, I am trying to read the relationship between two people at a nearby table. From the few words that cross the crowded din, and the clothing and body language, I guess that they are conservative, single, affluent, and do not know each other well. It seems that they are becoming less interested in each other as the evening, and the wine and talk, progress. At one point, I hear one force a laugh, definitely very forced, and then say, "Anyway . . . ," trailing off. Neither speaks for several minutes.

✹ ✹ ✹

One of my favourite places in the world, in my life, is the seawall walk around Stanley Park, especially the portion where you can see far into the watery distance, past the moored freighters and West Vancouver and the mountain, past the University of British Columbia and Wreck Beach point, into the edge of the sky.

On this weekend in Vancouver, I put on my sneakers and jogging shorts and two layers of T-shirts, and move around the 10 km wall, smelling the water and seaweed, welcoming the damp morning chill. There are so many parts to this walk, and as always these shift and vary depending on where my life is.

In the last few years I have developed a right leg limp,

leading people to ask me what I've done. I have no idea; it just drags a bit, that right leg, and won't lift as easily as it once did, to permit putting on a sock and shoe. It doesn't hurt, not at all, and I've grown used to the gait, attached to it, so now I don't even know if it is a real hitch or just some other new affectation, some psychic tic lurching out on my right lower side.

I could not care any less about my leg, as I slightly-limp around the seawall, counterclockwise, looking for truths and trees to bind with, avoiding tourist bicyclists and speeding roller-bladers, admiring most joggers, and trying to figure out what this place is trying to say to me or rather what I am trying to hear.

For almost three decades, I have been occasionally walking this seawall, fast or slow, alone or with others, dry or wet, early or late, and every time I experience a combined sense of fear and euphoria, a welcome dread. It doesn't keep me away, quite the opposite. Today, for some reason, I am determined not to leave-bad-enough-alone but instead to keep turning this over until I can see into it. In my pockets, I've got several chestnuts, just stripped from the fallen shells, gathered from the ground back on Haro Street, off Denman. I hold a couple of these as I walk, and I watch the water and the trees, looking for the shimmering lines of connection.

The closest I am able to come to dissecting the sensation of happy foreboding is to glimpse my departing shadow in the deep of the trees. If I were to ask someone to scatter my ashes around, this would be a fine place to do it, in back amongst some high wet trees, but definitely and always facing the water. The rain is much warmer, and my limping leg is comfortable.

I have a way to go before I'm home, but for now this will do just fine, with not a river in sight.

Sheep In
Sheep's Clothing

About a year ago I received a copy of the *Annals of the Royal College of Physicians and Surgeons of Canada*. I'm a physician, a specialist in Community Medicine (what the rest of the non-Canadian world calls "public health"), and my fees are paid, so I receive the *Annals*. This copy arrived on a day when I was feeling distinctly fed up with the state and role of "public health" in Ontario, in particular, and Canada, in general. My fed-up-ness was based on an increasing in-my-face realization that working towards the collective health of the population in a non-egalitarian society addicted to free-wheeling consumerism and to the selfish perpetuation of individual choice might be counter-productive, useless, a waste of time. (There is a slight chance that this perception was also based on my being a chronic malcontent, but I'll ignore that possibility.) The *Annals* called for submissions to the upcoming annual meeting of the Royal College, the fraternity of medical specialists, to be held in Vancouver. I dashed off a mildly vitriolic half-page rant titled "Community Medicine: Just

Another Brick in the Wall" and felt considerably better by the doing. (Purging continues to be therapeutic.) The abstract was short and blunt, and read as follows:

In 1947 the World Health Organization proclaimed the obvious, namely that there is more to health than the absence of illness. A succession of passionate iconoclasts have followed with their takes on the immense intricacy of *community* health and the mostly futile population health efforts of illness care providers. Fifty years after 1947, we are still in search of the obvious, which is that illness care is needed for those who are ill, and to have a healthy public requires something completely different.

Public health practice in Canada goes under the title of Community Medicine, which begs key questions: What is "community," according to whom, and to what purpose? And what does this have to do with "medicine"? Instead of focusing on issues of social justice and the interactive aspects of society that promote health—such as employment, equity, shared values, and inter-dependence—Community Medicine in most of Canada has accepted the neo-conservative agenda. The result has been a fearful and somewhat cynical emphasis on illness, rather than health promotion and social advocacy.

Community Medicine has retreated and, as a result, has become just another obstacle to community health. We have circled back to seeing health as the absence of illness, as evidenced by the growing size of the immunization and tobacco-prevention eggs in our shrinking basket. These are necessary but not sufficient. We righteously proclaim tobacco to be the number one preventable cause of illness in our society, ignoring poverty, and, by extension, ignoring health.

Walt Kelly's "Pogo" had it right: we have found the enemy, and it is us.

Let me provide some background: I went into medicine in the 1960s, seeing it as a possible route towards interpersonal caring and social usefulness, and I trained in public health in the 1980s, thinking it would be a progressive and political arm of a conservative profession, leading towards social justice and citizen-based science. It appears, in double retrospect, that naiveté and stupidity are close relatives and that I am my own first cousin.

The abstract I'd submitted to the Royal College was accepted, and I groaned when I realized what a masochistic little nightmare I'd set up. John Last, editor of the *Annals*, as well as editor and author of multiple other influential journals, books, texts, presentations, letters-to-the-editor, and conversations with God, sent me a cryptic, handwritten note, attached to the form acceptance letter, saying, "As a Community Medicine specialist myself, I was especially pleased to see this abstract!" There was a definite possibility that the jury of my peers was going to be seriously pissed off.

In order to prepare for the anticipated uninhibited negative response to my traitorous carping, I took some annual leave and visited a few BC places new to me, flying to Edmonton and then taking the 21-hour bus from Edmonton to Prince Rupert, a ferry through the Inside Passage to Port Hardy on Vancouver Island, the meandering bus to Nanaimo, and a quick ferry to Vancouver, having days to sit and collect images along the way.

Antidotes, by definition, are more powerful than poison, and I was intent on getting the therapeutic mix just right. In Vancouver I walked through the rain, circled

Stanley Park's seawall several times, bought smoked salmon at Granville Island, checked off excellent restaurants in the snobbish *Where To Eat In Canada*, gathered pockets full of chestnuts from the ground on a side street near Denman, and explored acceptable home truths with an old friend. Poison be damned, self-induced or otherwise; I was on a roll of my own baking.

On the day of the presentation, I asked myself what I was really trying to accomplish here and received an internally incoherent response, not for the first time. I remembered a similar situation, several years before, when my medicine-must-be-*more* presentation was followed by a pointed direction from one of the doctors in the audience, telling me, "If you don't like what we're doing, why don't you do us all a favour and leave; go do something else." This was followed by a nasty ripple of pointed applause. Medical types are *so* sensitive, at least regarding the issues of power and status.

The Vancouver presentation itself was brief, about fifteen minutes, quite dry, and was met with polite applause by the forty or so small-room attendees. I braced for some pointed and hostile comments, telegraphed (my paranoid radar said) by several faces. John Last was in the front row and was first to his feet, complimenting me on my analysis, and inviting me to send him a copy of the talk, for publication in the *Annals*. If there had been any tendency in the room to hoist me ever so high on my own rhetorical petard, it vanished with his mischievous verbal alliance. I don't know if I would otherwise have received a rough ride, but I can live in ignorance, an ongoing defense.

The flight home to Kenora was uneventful, anticlimactic even. I kept thinking about the middle-aged wheezer who had slogged by me on the 10-km Stanley

Park seawall, bare-chested and red-faced in the cold September rain, living in vain hope, but for how long?

It appears that we all dig our own traps, and then adroitly maneuver our way out, a species of rock-rolling Sisyphus. (It's a living.)

Stories

"...the worst thing about regret is that it makes you duck the chance of suffering new regret just as you get a glimmer that nothing's worth doing unless it has the potential to fuck up your whole life."
—Richard Ford,
in *Independence Day*

"The larger loneliness of our lives evolves from our unwillingness to spend ourselves, stir ourselves."
—Carol Shields,
in *The Stone Diaries*

Flatwater Brook

The Labrador Airways mail plane, a red and white single-engine Otter on wheels and skis, taxied away from the Goose Bay terminal. It was 8 am, a quiet cold February morning with an edge of red dawn still hanging on. The plane looked old and sounded older, chugging and seeming to strain. Bob MacDonald, RCMP Goose Bay detachment, sat in the co-pilot's seat, with blue nylon mailbags piled in the cabin behind, to the roof. He did not mind the age or sound of the plane, in fact felt it to be sane and efficient. Bob MacDonald was glad to be there, in early Labrador daylight, in a plane that had been known to fly. He knew Etien Rich, the pilot, and Rich had made room, since the regular passenger run to Rigolet didn't go for two more days and the RCMP plane was in Nain.

The Otter took its position at the end of the runaway, tiny and fragile looking in the middle of the long extra-wide WW II strip. The pilot checked the flaps and trim again, readjusted the fuel mix, and pushed the throttle ahead. The plane moved smoothly down the runway, roaring, and Bob could not tell the exact moment it left the ground. It gained altitude slowly, seeming to lift with its nose pointed slightly down for a few seconds. Then they turned east in a sweep over the airport's edge.

Bob could see that there was only one American military plane parked where there had been several the year before. Good to see them gone, he thought, then looked down at the town of Happy Valley and further out past the river to the village of Mud Lake, the houses scattered along islands and small channels. Happy Valley-Goose Bay, trying to be a city, he thought. The CBC radio station talked of "downtown Happy Valley-Goose Bay," which was in reality four streets in search of an intersection.

The area had been someone's berry patch before the Second World War led to the construction of the Goose Bay air base and the civilian town beside it, now called Happy Valley. Goose Bay had meant a change in the lives of many Labradorians, who had previously not worried about industries or roads or subsidies, and often not about comfort, only about need. They had lived in small scattered coastal and lake settlements, but since Goose Bay came along and then union with Canada in 1949, there had been a steady change toward larger centres. Happy Valley-Goose Bay waxed and waned, most recently riding the sonic-booms of NATO's low-level-flying obscenity.

Looking back Bob could see the river turning, frozen, into central Labrador, now called the Churchill, before that the Hamilton, and before that the Grand. He turned away from the river and thought of it going back, past Gull Island, up to Grand Falls site, now the Churchill Falls hydro dam.

Bob had been posted at Goose Bay for a year, and when the realignment of coastal responsibilities had occurred, with the coastal Cartwright detachment passing

Rigolet over to Goose Bay, he had applied for the "post," which meant visiting Rigolet once a month. MPY, the RCMP Otter, usually took him in and out, and he'd been there for three visits so far. The Cartwright Mounties had not been eager to visit Rigolet and had usually managed to go only every couple of months, and then often just for the day.

Bob had been thinking of leaving the Force, not talking of it or making plans but just accepting the fact that he was unhappy. He found much of the work petty, demeaning either to himself or to the people he was dealing with. He had never been able to accept the fact that most people now disliked or feared him on sight, because of the yellow leg stripes, and in response he had often been even more aloof and unyielding than the situation, or the law, demanded. He had begun to dislike the people, the "public." But he became more open, and occasionally even warm, when he started going to Rigolet.

Even before Rigolet he had noticed that Labrador had its hold on him, that he loved the feel of the cold in the snow and the air, the trips on ski-doo to North West River or The Islands or just off in the woods, and the view of the spruce and lakes stretching back and back from the height of MPY. Occasionally he had been able to talk with some of the older people in Goose Bay, about how they had lived only a few years before. He would ask about the ordinary details, the building of the cabin, the getting of water and wood, the spring fishing and winter freeze-up, but usually his job made it impossible for the necessary ease and friendliness ever to get started.

In Rigolet the feeling had been different. He had made a good initial decision in choosing not to stay at the Hudson's Bay manager's house, as the other Mounties had.

He remembered standing on the Rigolet pond as MPY left him the first day, asking people on ski-doos if they'd take him into the village. And did they know anyone he could stay with?

"Mounties most always stay with the manager," one man told him.

"Anywhere else I can stay?" Bob asked. No one had said anything, but a young man motioned him to sit on a komatik, and then delighted in giving a wild and jolting ride for the mile into Rigolet. Should've given the son-of-a-bitch a ticket for reckless driving, Bob thought, smiling as he remembered his efforts to hold on in a dignified manner, in the best tradition of the Force. The man had finally stopped in the middle of the village, grinning, and Bob thanked him, grinning back. He had walked around the town, with his small brown bag, seeing the 40 or so homes, the old square Hudson's Bay store, the Power House with its heavy pushing generator whine, and the school set off from the houses, facing the shallow bay. He had gone toward the school, feeling conspicuous and foreign and lonely.

Kids had been coming out, and he went up the steps, asking one of them what the teacher's name was.

"Which one?" said the kid.

"The nicest one," said Bob, thinking he might regret this later.

"Lilly; she's our teacher," the boy said.

He had gone in and looked around the hallway when a short, round-faced woman came out of a room and smiled a real smile at him. "Hello," said Lilly.

"Hi," said Bob, "I'm looking for a place to stay and don't know who to ask."

"You can stay at our place," said Lilly, without hesitation.

"You'll have to sleep with the radio in back, but you're welcome to stay."

So he had, each visit, and had relearned how to just sit and talk and relax with people, with many seeming to forget the yellow stripe on his leg, unless it became relevant, which was seldom. He had stayed from two to five days each time, getting "caught" by snow twice, and had had to explain to Staff Sergeant Williamson why a day visit was no longer adequate. He made the explanation vague, emphasizing the public relations aspect of the visits and avoiding specific details of his work. This was accepted, more or less.

So he was going back today and felt good about it. The Otter moved east, over frozen Lake Melville and toward the Labrador Sea. The sun was glinting hard on the flat tops of the Mealy Mountains, which lined the south shore of the lake. Bob loved this, seeing the narrow sculpted glare of the two-hundred-kilometre-long frozen lake, with Mokami Hill on the left, north of the lake, and still further north White Bear Mountain sweeping up out of the spruce.

Today he could see a ski-doo and komatik going from North West River toward the Islands. He remembered the man in Goose Bay telling how he and several others had walked from Makkovik to Goose in the early war years, when there was work to be had on the Base. They had walked out in the fall, after freeze-up, carrying very little and hunting-fishing their food, over 250 miles. Then back again in spring, before break-up.

As they approached the end of Lake Melville and Rigolet, Bob could see the open water of the Inlet, with steam rising off it in the cold of the morning. Etien banked the plane over the village, circling twice to let the people know it was here. A very rough airstrip, a bare-bones Nursing Station, and a temperamental phone, TV, and radio system, thought Bob, at the same time disgusted with the provincial government's lack of resources or concern, and yet revelling in the elite privacy of the place. Etien turned the plane toward the small pond, lowered the skis and adjusted fuel mix, throttle and flaps again.

The plane eased down and bumped along on the snow, which was wind-blown hard. Almost as soon as they had stopped and Etien had shut down the engine, several ski-doos came out to greet them. One had a large komatik, for the mailbags, and there was a man holding on tightly in the komatik box. He was out quickly, bundled in hat and scarves and thick pants, looking anxious and asking Etien to take him back to Goose Bay.

"Job tells me bad weather's coming," he said, "and I've got to get back."

Bob looked over at Job, who was loading the mailbags into the komatik, and Job, hearing every word of the Social Services man's plea, caught Bob's eye and winked. A shared mocking. Ever fearful of being "stuck," the visitors would come and go to the coast as quickly as possible, always with an eye on the weather and a plane. The coastal people were used to this scene, perhaps pleased by it. It was a test. Most visitors couldn't cope with the absence of movie and highway, bar and hospital, and the key fact that often there was no possible exit.

Etien motioned Social Services into the co-pilot's seat, and Bob climbed on a ski-doo behind the same man who had first taken him into town, three months before. The airport bus, he thought, and said, "Jake, go slower this time will you? I'm getting older every day." Jake smiled again, and they went in, slowly.

✳ ✳ ✳

Toby Wilson was staying at Lilly and Alf Pottles'. This was his second visit. He was living in Nain for the winter, but a part of his job was to visit all the coastal communities. Toby was the obligatory northern anthropologist, or at least most people who needed a label, a reference point, would have listed him as that. He had finished his Masters work at Memorial University but needed to write a thesis. This year's work, funded by the university and supervised by LOPA, the Labrador Original Peoples Association, had started out as "fieldwork" for this thesis, but it wasn't going well. At least the fieldwork wasn't; he felt that the living of his life was going *very* well.

He hated to think of himself as an anthropologist, being careful to define himself only as Toby. He supposed that most people did not feel this way but instead enjoyed their static roles, searched for them, needing the security. In spite of this, he usually read books relevant to social sciences, a phrase he mocked, and was now reading *Pedagogy of the Oppressed* for the third time. This time he was sure he truly "saw" what Freire was after and how clearly it applied to the colonized and oppressed Labrador people. He had taken up their cause.

Toby hated the feel and form of surveys, withdrawing from the organization they required, the adopting of roles and questions, and the resulting space between himself and the people. He feared that space; it had plagued and followed him before. Toby did not consider that this space, this lack of connection, might be a common thing. He would talk with the people, in their homes, visiting often and trying to enter easily with charm and smiles and passionate talk, always with the words. And often this seemed to work, as the people became used to him. But he was never quite sure.

The arrangement with the university and LOPA, with one funding and the other supervising, left him accountable to no one. As a result he had spent the last six months sitting in people's kitchens, drinking tea and beer, talking and listening, trying to find a pattern. He was alive and fuming with unfocused ideas and moral energy.

The stay at Alf and Lilly's was pleasant. Alf was out looking after his traps. "He likes to be out in the country," Lilly had said to Toby, not mentioning that Alf usually left immediately on the arrival of any stranger.

✳ ✳ ✳

Jake stopped his ski-doo in front of Alf and Lilly's, and Bob got off the back of the ski-doo. He went in the front door and saw a short, heavy man in his late 20s or early 30s, sitting at the kitchen table, wearing blue jeans, deer skin moccasins, and a high-necked sweater with zigzag red and green designs. He had long and untrimmed beard and hair, both red-brown, and he gave Bob the usual "what-the-hell-do-*you*-want, cop?" look. Toby had looked up to see a tall, skinny man, mid to late thirties, wearing a blue parka, beaver skin cap, and yellow leg stripes.

"Shit," Toby thought, especially as he saw the appraising and unfriendly look Bob had given him.

"Shit," Bob thought.

"Hi," Toby said, "Have some tea?" and smiled, the disarming smile.

"Thanks," Bob said, "Anyone home?"

"Just me."

"Lilly or Alf?"

"Alf's out at his traps, and Lilly's in school. Come on in."

"OK," said Bob, resenting the host attitude. He put his bag down and took off his parka and hat. "You visiting?," he asked.

"Yeah, my name's Toby Wilson; live in Nain. I'm working for LOPA, usually stay here when I'm in Rigolet."

"I'm Bob MacDonald. You from Newfoundland?"

"No. Nova Scotia, Halifax. You?"

"Pictou. There's a lot of us around."

They had tea and talked about ice and winds. Toby did most of the talking, retreating into verbal glitter to avoid awkwardness. Bob retreated into silence.

Lilly came home at noon. She smiled at Bob and said, "You come on the mail plane?" She rarely called him Bob even though he requested it, not really agreeing that a Mountie should be called by his first name. It seemed to undermine the whole purpose of the thing.

"Toby's got the back room," she said, "you'll have to bunk on the couch; that OK?"

He was grateful for the couch, the space.

"Two Nova Scotians," Lilly said, "Did you know each other before?" They looked at each other and both couldn't help smiling at that. "I don't think we'd met, had we Bob?" said Toby. They hadn't, they agreed.

After lunch Bob had to go out to see some people.

"I don't suppose I could come along, could I?" asked Toby, sounding surprisingly unassured and young to both of them.

"Sure," said Bob, also surprised at himself. "There's one or two people I might have to see alone, but I'll tell you." They walked around the town. The wind had come up, and clouds were moving in from the east.

"East wind," said Toby, "you could be here for a few days." A test, this was.

"I hope so," said Bob, passing easily.

They walked toward the Hudson's Bay store sitting out on the point, old, made of wood, white and red trim, with two sheds, a house and wharf nearby, and a boardwalk angled in to the front door. Toby started talking, feeling fine walking in the wind.

"The most useful thing that store has to offer is a snapshot of itself, from the outside. If you want cigarettes or pop or chips or bars, it's a fine place, an emporium in fact, but if you happen to be one of those unlucky ones needing such things as meat or vegetables or fruit or milk, forget it. Some years even the canned stuff runs out, in May or June months, before the boats come, but that's only some years, and there's usually lots of partridges and rabbits those years, so it's OK. Maybe the Bay and whoever supplies partridges and rabbits have an arrangement, but that's only speculation. The fact is that the Bay *looks* good, and I for one am always thankful to see it there." The people who saw them going by saw two outsiders walking toward the store, laughing.

Toby talked as they went around the village, and Bob soon knew the outline of his story, which was very different from his own. Toby's parents worked in Halifax and he had grown up there in what Bob imagined, accurately, to be a large house with two cars. Toby had played a lot of games, with some skill, and had spent six years in university. Bob also had a history, a background, but he felt that he wasn't in retreat from his as much as Toby was. Toby's tone seemed to indicate a fear of his past, and Bob didn't understand that.

Alf was home when they returned. He was a large, shy

man and didn't enjoy the chatter and scrutiny of visitors. He had to come home today because a storm was on the way. He tapped the barometer as he came in the door and watched the needle dip.

"Damn," he thought, as he saw Bob and Toby come toward the house, "*two* of them," but he wasn't all that unhappy about it. Toby could make him laugh, with his talk and wild stories, and Bob seemed to be from somewhere similar to Rigolet.

Lilly asked Bob, during supper, where he was from and what his family was like. This was the first time anything like this had been asked here, and he chose to try to answer it, not to deflect it.

"From Pictou, Nova Scotia; have you been to Nova Scotia?" They hadn't.

"Pictou is a small town, smaller than Goose Bay, on a harbour, right across from a pulp mill now, but that wasn't there when I was a kid. My father was a salesman, pots and pans, hammers and tools, metalware. My mother worked at home." Bob noticed that everyone was listening, carefully.

"That a good job, your father's?" Alf asked.

"Not very good, at least not for him. He hated it. We had enough food and clothes and things, but a couple of years were not good. There's a lot of people out of work in Nova Scotia now, same as here."

"Do you go back much?" Lilly asked.

"Yes, a lot. It's home," said Bob, and saw Toby look away with obvious annoyance.

Toby immediately began to outline his solutions for "regional disparity," linking them with Labrador. Alf had heard outsiders expound on Labrador for years, and he soon moved into the other room and smoked a cigarette.

He had once told Bob that it didn't really matter what outsiders said or did, because sooner or later they left, usually sooner. Lilly listened as Toby became angrier and angrier at the evils of the colonial system in Labrador, the racist exploitation of Indian and Inuit lands, and the need for immediate change and local take-over. She wondered what he must think of them, with all these things wrong, then and now. Bob talked, in response, about his life in Nova Scotia, having to work hard as a teenager, of seeing the RCMP as a way out of a corner, and being grateful for it.

"Grateful!" said Toby, and the word brought quick contempt to his face.

Bob told Toby of the people in Pictou County, Guysborough County, the south shore, driving to Halifax to work, and working hard, not asking for land claims or free drugs or anything they couldn't earn for themselves.

"Or take for themselves," added Toby, and he talked of aboriginal rights and Freire and oppression.

They didn't hear much of what the other said, going their own ways, following their own truths. They kept talking, neither delivering any hard verbal shots, even though there had been openings.

Lilly and Alf sat in the living room, talking to a nephew. They didn't have children and a lot of people visited. The voices went on in the kitchen.

❋ ❋ ❋

The next day it snowed and blew, a whipping wind that moved fine-snow level to the ground and into drifts by houses. Bob walked past the store and along the bank of the narrow inlet, where the water was open all winter, watching the snow being driven into the water. The wind was going through most things, including Bob. The drifts were high enough to make him duck under some wires and clotheslines. Most houses used wood stoves, and piles of dry spruce logs were stacked, the logs leaning against each other like multi-dimensional A's without the bar. His first time on the coast Bob had thought they were teepee frames, from a distance, but had had the sense to keep his mouth shut. The telephone, which was in Alf and Lilly's back bedroom, was "out," with only static floating in from Goose Bay.

On Bob's third day in Rigolet, he and Toby walked out to the Pond and back, with the snow and wind still coming strong from the east. They were relaxing with each other, although both would have been offended and incredulous to realize that people were seeing them as similar entities.

The snow had held for three days, and even when it stopped, the wind blew hard enough to keep the planes from coming.

"Blowing a gale," Alf said. He was restless from days of being at home, with strangers in the house and too much talk.

Bob, Alf and Toby were sitting at the kitchen table in the evening, now with very little talk or movement. Bob had called Goose Detachment that day, and even though telephone reception was poor, he understood that the RCMP plane was still sitting in Nain, wind blowing around it. The corporal he had spoken to said that even when it got back to Goose, MPY had to make a trip to Cartwright before picking up Bob. On one other trip Bob and Alf had talked, cautiously, about Bob joining Alf out in the country for a few days.

"Alf, how would you feel about a ski-doo trip to

Cartwright? A cruise. Wind or no wind, tomorrow say."

Alf laughed and said yes, and Toby and Bob were out of the house in five minutes to try to rent a ski-doo and a komatik, the sled pulled behind the machine. Alf tapped the barometer and then started to get his things together. They were moving.

Later on in the evening Toby and Bob came back, on ski-doo.

"$20 a day; not bad. Good machine too. No komatik though, Alf. Can you take all our stuff on yours?"

"No sweat," said Alf grinning, moving in his slow, large, graceful way, gathering up extra socks, candles, filling the grub-box, finding new komatik lashing.

Toby said he had to go out for a few minutes and asked Bob if he wanted to come. A reciprocal move. They cut through the wind and over the drifts to Peter and Mary Shiwak's, a small house in a hollow, now well buried in snow, with an overhanging porch that made them duck as they went in. Peter and Mary had lived around Lake Melville all their lives, over 70 years. Their house was warm, with an old Ensign wood stove burning fast, crackling the dry spruce, kettle steaming to the back. The stove was ancient and had "United Nail and Foundry—St. John's" on the draft at the front. They sat for a while, with Toby seeming the most at ease of anyone. He asked Mary Shiwak if she would like to go to Cartwright with him, on ski-doo, that he was looking for company.

"I would," she said. "That would be a good trip."

"You'll have to share a sleeping bag with me," Toby said, flashing a well-executed inoffensive grin.

"I'm not going that way," she said. "It's warmer here."

They all laughed, more relaxed now, and Bob saw what Toby was trying to tell him, that he did care for the people and not just for abstract ideas of them. Bob wondered if Toby was also trying to show that the people cared for him. They walked home, wind on their backs this time, a "fair wind."

Alf was up at 5 am, still getting things ready. Lilly was up at 6, and she was not impressed by Bob's windpants. "Simpson-Sears," she said, the ultimate scornful epithet. She then supervised Bob's borrowing of an extra pair of Alf's pants. Toby was fending for himself, happy, "doing fine," he said.

Alf's komatik held the large grub-box, tent and stove, snowshoes, and Bob's bag, all overlapped with old brown canvas and lashed tightly. Bob was to sit on the grub-box, and Alf tied a large piece of thick felt to the box, for comfort and for holding on. By 8 am the sun was breaking through, with the wind from the southeast, "still blowing some," Alf said. The trip now had a life of its own, a time, and there was no thought of waiting for planes. Alf had a shotgun across his back as he checked the machine for the last time.

They left Rigolet, having to circle the open water of the Inlet by going about 10 miles west, up Lake Melville toward Goose Bay, before cutting across the Lake and turning south. They all had their parkas fully tied around their faces in the cold morning, and were wearing heavy boots, gloves and pants. Toby noticed how much newer his and Bob's gear was, and that Alf seemed very much at home in his clothes and on the ski-doo.

They went 10 miles with Alf going slowly, and Bob and Toby looking around, trying to keep pace with the water, trees and hills. There was no keeping pace. At Carwallow Hill Alf speeded up to try to make it to the top, even with the load, and Bob, not paying attention, was catapulted neatly into a drift as they rounded a turn. Alf came back and made sure Bob was unbroken, with a glance, not saying anything but not annoyed, a kind person. Bob pushed on the komatik to get the ski-doo going up the hill and then walked up after letting Toby go by. Toby looked cold and happy. The two were waiting at the top of the hill; Carwallow, Bob said the name over to himself.

Alf said, "It took me eight hours to get over this one year. Left Rig'let at 6, got over this by about 3; deep new snow and had to push and pull the ski-doo the whole way. Bad hill." Going down the other side it was steep, opening out onto Lake Melville, with all the open water now behind them.

They went west on the lake's north shore for another mile or so, then cut across and returned east along the south shore. In order to reach the Backway, a long cul-de-sac arm of Lake Melville running southeast, they crossed a point of land with an open untreed area, flat snow, no wind, perfect going. There was a high flat rock face to their left, close to them and sheer, with spruce trees wedging roots into cracks and on ledges, at all angles. They came off the point and into the wind, on the Backway. The wind was stronger now and into their faces. It had sculpted the snow into hard sharp-edged waves along the frozen lake, giving Bob a jarring, slapping ride as the komatik was pulled off small snow-ledges, over and over. The price of admission, he thought, and was glad to pay.

They moved along, slowly, and after a half-hour or so, Alf stopped and turned off his machine, lifting the hood to cool it down. Toby and Bob jumped around to loosen their legs and the cold, to unbend their backs. Alf walked around, rubbing his left cheek, where he had a small white patch.

"Always get frostbit right there," he said.

Before they started off, Alf told them that there was a cabin up ahead, at Pease Cove, not very far. By the time they reached it, they were so cold it was painful to move. Snow had piled up against the door, sloped by the wind, and they scraped it away. There was wood in the box and a homemade stove, from an oil drum. The wood was dry, and in only a few minutes the stove was alive, red hot, and Alf had bread thawing near it, snow in his kettle on the stove, and a Carnation can opened and placed by the bread. He then opened up three tins of corned beef and lined them up by the bread and milk. The cabin was small, made of logs with moss-chinking, with the gables and the door and roof of plywood. It warmed up quickly. They didn't take off much though, shivering as the heat moved in on them.

"I'm perished with cold," Toby said.

The coffee and food were fine, and they hated to move. Alf went out and gassed up the machines, then came in and repacked the grub-box. Toby, watching everything, saw him cover the holes in the Carnation can with frozen butter, so it wouldn't spill in the box.

They left, jolting slowly up the Backway, staying near land in some places because Alf knew the ice might be bad. Alf was constantly watching the shore, and as they approached one point, he suddenly stopped, got off the ski-doo and moved toward the trees and willows. He took his gun from his back, aimed it at what seemed to Toby and Bob to be just a snowbank with a few very bare willows slanting out of it, waited a second, and fired. Several white birds suddenly rose up and flew off, but two stayed down.

"Willow Ptarmigan," said Toby, "white partridges; supper."

Alf had followed the birds, and they heard another shot from around the point. He came back with four Ptarmigan, heads flopping, small bloody holes in the white feathers. Alf tucked them under a flap of the brown canvas and started the machine.

They travelled the length of the Backway, about thirty miles, gradually crossing it, after they were well away from Pease Cove. The wind still blew at them, into them, but the food and heat had eased the cold, and they were all right. A plane went over the Mealies, high to be out of the wind, toward Cartwright. They couldn't hear it. Toby gave the thumbs up and a grin to Bob, looking at the plane.

At about 3:30 they turned off the Backway, now moving east toward the ocean, across land by a series of small frozen ponds and creeks and marshes, toward West Bay. The daylight was gold, coming in on an angle from behind them, as the sun slowly eased down. Alf took them over a little rise and then up beside an old cabin. They stopped the machines. "Right over there's a good place for the night," he said, pointing to a small clearing in the trees, away from the wind. They all went into the cabin. Alf said that he hadn't been here for years, that Mercer Roberts used to live there, alone, but now lived in Cartwright, with his nephew. The cabin was made of large squared timbers, but people had been sawing off bits from the porch and around the broken windows, for firewood, as they passed.

The place was called Flatwater Brook, said Alf. "Shame to see it beaten up."

While Toby and Bob found standing dead spruce for firewood, Alf put the tent up, with fir boughs thick on the floor, and the small tin stove inside with the pipe out through an opening. He propped the ski-doos up on sticks, so the tracks were off the snow, rolled the komatik on its side, and brought the grub-box in. The grey-blue light of twilight came and went slowly, as the sun angled away gradually. Alf found some dry wood of his own and had the fire going and the tent warm when Bob and Toby got back with two large sticks of wood each. While they split stove lengths, he put three cans of sardines on the stove, and the kettle full of snow, and began to pluck the birds. Bob and Toby brought in the wood, and Alf put three of the split and cleaned birds into a pot of boiling water, adding salt and pork scraps.

"It'll be a couple of hours before that's ready," he told them, stoking up the tin stove and lighting a candle, which he put in a holder on the grub-box. They spread Alf's heavy sleeping bag over the boughs, as a rug, and tied the tent door shut, gradually removing clothes. The wind seemed to be high and behind them, in treetops, not touching the tent. They ate the sardines to take an edge off the hunger, drank some tea and waited on the partridges. Alf smoked a cigarette, Toby read a book by the candle, and Bob watched the stove flame through the damper hole.

"I could live here," Bob said.

Alf looked at him, and said, "It's hard." Toby didn't say anything.

They ate carefully, being grateful to the partridges, who would have preferred they had gone hungry, Toby thought. The meal was excellent, the tent was warm, and they ached and were tired. They talked awhile, with Toby and Alf asking Bob about Mountie training in Saskatchewan, both fascinated but from different angles.

"We don't have horse work anymore," Bob told them, "Haven't had for years." Later, he told of going into a barber after a month's holidays, with longer hair and a beard, and the barber had said, "You're in the Force, eh?"

"How did he know?" Bob asked, amazed and embarrassed still, and Toby and Alf smiled.

Alf answered their questions about his childhood in Lake Melville, near Pearl River, and about his time trapping in the Mealy Mountains. The wind continued to move in the spruce and fir behind their tent, whining and then sighing, almost removed from them. They talked for a long while, like friends.

Neither Toby nor Bob had sleeping bags, but Alf had brought blankets. He told them not to worry, that he would keep the fire going. Whenever one of them woke up in the night, Alf was sitting, stoking the stove or smoking a cigarette, and the tent was warm.

Alf woke them up in the morning by making breakfast. The wind had dropped out. They ate bread and molasses and canned fish and coffee, then packed up and were soon ready to leave. The sun was in their faces, and the going was better over the ponds and frozen marshes. Without the wind and with the smoother ride, it was a different world, a different day. It took only about an hour to reach the water, at West Bay, where the Labrador Sea comes in from the Atlantic. They stopped on a rise of land, a cliff, turned off the machines and looked out over the water. It was grey and heavy looking, even in the sun, with slow inconclusive swells because of the slob-ice near the shore.

About 15 miles from Cartwright a man came down over the bank ahead of them, taking long careful steps in his oval snowshoes. He was a short, thin man, with a gun over one shoulder and an axe and steel traps over the other. Alf pulled over toward him, turned off the motor, and said, "Where's your machine, Henry?"

"Can't get one this winter, too dear they are now, and

the gas; don't need it. The old one won't go anymore."
The man didn't take the axe, traps or gun from his
shoulders.

"You walk from Cartwright?" Alf asked.

"Yeah. You on a cruise, or what?"

"Yeah. Taking the Mountie here to Cartwright," Alf
said, gesturing at Bob.

"See Mercer's place?"

"It's not so good. You want a ride?"

"No. I've got some more traps to get. Fox is cute this
year. Not a one today."

"See you."

They drove on, taking the Mountie to Cartwright,
Bob and Toby both thought. Bob looked back at Henry
walking on along and saw that Toby was watching him too.

Alf seemed in a hurry to get to Cartwright, and they
didn't stop to boil-up, just kept moving, all very relaxed
and warm enough in the sun; easygoing. A flock of black
ducks, a big flock, rose out of the icy water ahead of them
and circled, to land well behind them.

They moved fast across the strait to Cartwright, not
sure where the bad ice was, and came up over a rise to the
houses of the town, moving between them to the harbour.
Bob was startled to see MPY fueling up at the Lab Airways
gas drums and pointed it out to Alf. He led the way across
the harbour to the white and blue plane.

"Hi, Joe," Bob said to the pilot, "You just get in?"

"Bob? I thought you were in Rigolet. No, got in late
yesterday afternoon. Going to Goose now."

"Room for me?"

"All kinds. We're going in about an hour. Come on up
to the station for some coffee. You look frozen."

Toby and Alf decided that they would rather go find a

place to stay, instead of having coffee with the RCMP. Bob got his bag and awkwardly tried to pay Alf for the trip but was refused. He gave some money to Toby to give Alf for gas and food, and watched them drive across the harbour, wondering where they would spend the night. Alf was leading, Toby following, kneeling on his ski-doo seat, both looking very much at home. Bob went up to the detachment for a coffee, remembering as he went that he still had Alf's windpants.

As MPY flew over the Mealy Mountains toward Goose Bay, Bob looked off to the northeast, trying to find the ski-doo trail they had made. He realized clearly that some changes were due. "Taking the Mountie here to Cartwright," he thought, and wondered what he could do to make a living in Rigolet.

Solving Problems

Stella Keefe was sitting at her kitchen table, alone in her
three-room house, looking at the small, partly frosted window and imagining the wind making its own ghosts on the
harbour. She didn't hear the kettle boiling on the stove.

Her mind was sliding back and forth between the
problem she had to deal with now and an image of herself
and her husband George moving across that same harbour,
jumping on and off the dog-pulled komatik as they helped
each other and the animals, with the children in the sled
box blanket-wrapped and open-eyed, watching. Four of
the six children were now dead, and she kept her mind well
clear of that. George had died eight years ago, lying still
beside her in their bed when she woke in the morning,
with mucous on his face and in his mouth. His eyes had
been open, clearly staring at the water stain on the ceiling
over their heads. Stella had dampened a cloth in the water
bucket and wiped George's face, carefully tucked the blankets around his neck, and tried to close his eyes and
mouth. His mouth wouldn't stay closed, and George
would have hated that.

After starting the fire in the stove and putting the kettle on, she had phoned for Jim, their youngest son, who lived next door. Jim was now a central part of the problem, because he and his wife Alice wanted Stella to move in with them, mainly because they knew they *had* to want it, that she needed help just to live. They loved her but were fully separate from the reality of her, her folds of thin wrinkled skin and the layers of old familiar clothes, even on the warmest day, her need for the sound of the wood stove and refusal to drink tap water, and the night confusion and terror that gripped her if she slept anywhere but in her own bed, George's bed. For the last eight years, Stella had avoided being taken out of that bed by sheer stubborn willfulness but now saw that she might not be able to win much longer.

One of the nurses, the rough unkind one who apparently thought Stella was deaf and stupid, was raising the question of the "old folks' home" in the city, and the Community Council chairman had even been over. He was a silly puffed-up nasty ass, Stella had thought as she watched him, watched his hands and eyes and mouth, all the telling parts. He'd made a mess of his father's business and now was doing the same with the town's business. He and even Jim had talked about her as if she wasn't in the same room at the same table, *her* room and table, George's room and table. George would have told them both, even Jim, to get out of their house and by the sweet Christ to do it fast, and they would have gone, without a word. She shook her head, angry with George for dying; he shouldn't have left. The chairman and Jim glanced over but didn't speak to her, just paused.

Stella had sat and listened carefully, staring at the window that faced the harbour. The chairman, a hard man who laughed too loud and too often to mask his lifelong bitterness, had said to Jim, "You've got to do something. Right down here at the Bottom, with the wind in the winter and the water in the spring of the year, it's not a fit place to live."

"I can't *make* Mother move. This is her home; she doesn't want to come with Alice and me."

"Nurse and I've been talking, and there's a way to get her to move to the Old Folks'. She could visit you whenever you want."

Jim hadn't said anything, just moved his tea mug around in slow circles, and Stella had felt moved to fill it with good hot tea and to touch his shoulder, but she hadn't.

"I don't think so, Ira, not yet," Jim had finally said.

"You're not going to have a say much longer, Jim, so do what you can while you can." Ira had said this with his false red-faced smile, standing up and putting on his coat, leaving without putting his mug in the sink.

The empty mug sat with Jim and Stella for some minutes while they were at the table, not talking. Stella had always felt Jim to be one of her few allies in the world, in her life. He had listened to her as a child, treating her words with respect before he eventually went on to live his own way. He also had shown the ultimate kindness by staying alive, not adding his death to her clouding vision.

Now, alone in her kitchen, Stella finally heard the boiling kettle, and she got up to make tea. As she poured the water over the bags into the brown teapot she heard George laugh behind her, the deep full laugh he had when he was about to reach around her from behind and touch her breasts, or when they both had shared some happy view that again confirmed their connection. She turned quickly to welcome him, finally, and fell on her side, breaking her left hip and spilling the boiling water over her right lower leg. The pain and the loneliness moved through her seconds later, but a separate watchful part of her knew that her problem had just been solved. She was glad George had been there to help.

Jim had found his mother semi-conscious on her kitchen floor several hours later, and had called the Nursing Station. The nurse told him to bring Stella ("Aunt Stella" she had said, using the local term) to the Station, saying there was nothing she could do in the home. Jim had picked Stella up as carefully as he could, with Alice there by then to help, and as they wrapped his mother with blankets in the komatik box he had quietly cursed everyone's stupidity.

"Why couldn't she live with us, and why can't that nurse see that just having her here would be a help?"

Even though the breeze was starting to move around to come in from the east, sure to bring bad weather, it was still clear and cold, about 20° below. They moved slowly across the harbour, the ski-doo pulling Stella and Alice in the sled box, with every bump wrenching all three.

At the Station, Jim heard the nurse in the clinic room speaking loudly to his mother and heard the difficulty and pain of undressing and examining her. He and Alice sat in the waiting room with their coats on, not talking, looking at their hands and boots. After a long while the nurse came in and said, "Your mother's broken her hip. It was sure to happen with her all alone in that shack. She's also got a bad burn on her right leg. What did she do?"

Jim said he didn't know. He and Alice didn't look at each other, feeling that the nurse was right, they should have prevented this.

"Well, she'll have to go to hospital. I'm going to call Dr. Robinson, and I've given her something for the pain. They'll come for her right away."

"Wind's shifting to the east, Miss," Jim had said. "Can we go in?"

Jim and Alice sat by the bed, with the Demerol now easing Stella into a sleep, looking at the traction on her left leg and the thick bandaging on her right leg. They heard the nurse phone the hospital. "I've got an 82-year-old woman who fell at home tonight and must have knocked some boiling water on herself as she went down. I think there's a fractured left hip and a full thickness burn from her right knee to the foot. I've got an IV going and gave her some Demerol. Can you come get her? I've got no one here to escort." The hospital would send a plane in the morning, with a nurse escort.

✼ ✼ ✼

Etien Rich flew the small green and white helicopter, call sign HAB, east from Goose Bay over the Mealy Mountains toward the south Labrador coast. He had a nurse on board, with a stretcher and all her gear, and he was flying this med-evac because the hospital plane was stuck north in a storm. That plane was a turbo-Beaver, and Etien had flown it for two years before going over to helicopters, so he knew the med-evac drill. He glanced at the nurse escort, sitting in the co-pilot's seat, and realized he didn't know her name. She was a small woman, English he supposed from her accent, and the huge parka that she wore made her look childish, overwhelmed, until you looked at her face. She had strong features, a careful face, Etien thought, and she was looking around as they flew, at the mountains and the instruments, at his hands, studying it all. Etien pointed to the co-pilot's set of headphones hanging by her head, and she put them on. They could talk now without shouting.

"I missed your name, sorry. I seem to hear faces, not the words," Etien said.

"Gill."

"Where are you from?"

"Right here, now. England before, just outside London. And Scotland for my midwifery. Also Australia to work. You?"

"Nova Scotia, the French Shore. I've been up here for almost ten years. How about you?"

"Six months."

"Like it?"

Gill paused and then asked him his name, knowing it already but not wanting to admit that.

"Etty—Etty Rich."

"Etty?"

"Etien, really. I get Etty, even Eddy."

"Do you like 'Etty' better?" she asked, looking right at his face for the first time. He was older than most of the pilots she had met, probably mid-thirties, tall with a thin face and dark eyes that seemed distant until he looked at you. His hands had several sets of scrapes and bruises, and short nails that were clean. The hands seemed to fit the controls. Gill had concentrated on his hands as they lifted off, as this was her first helicopter ride, and moving between wires and over poles as they left the hospital grounds scared her. She again focused on Etien's hands whenever the actuality of their distance up in the air, and the potential closeness of her death, moved in on her. She didn't think 'Etty' suited him, but maybe that was the point.

"No, I don't," Etien said, a bit surprised at the question, and relieved, because she had seemed so cool, so separate from her surroundings and the flight. "I like 'Etien' better, but most people seem to find it too formal."

"Especially men?"

"Yes, I guess so," he said, hearing the casual bias in her question but agreeing anyway; agreeing completely, in fact.

They flew a while more without talking, and then Gill took off the headphones and hung them up. OK, thought Etien. Separately, they watched the cut and flow of white, mostly frozen rivers, only open and steaming at a rapids, and the clumps and finger-runs of spruce and fir, these islands of green in the midst of white, where the snow had defined everything. Even though a wind had picked up and moved around to come from the east and was pushing heavy cloud toward them from out over the northern Labrador Sea, there was still the bright ungiving gold of early morning sun, seeming to be frozen tight to the ground. In the air this winter sun was on their faces, as the helicopter flew lower and lower, following rivers through the sloped edge of the Mealy Mountains, angling toward the coast.

When they landed at the Nursing Station, the weather was already starting to worsen.

"Can you make it?" Joe, the man who gassed up the machine, asked Etien. "It's coming down quick."

"I can't get back to Goose; this stuff has moved in from northeast, but I can still go south if we've got to, and get to the other hospital. Or we can sit here and wait it out. I'd rather do that."

The Station nurse told Gill and Etien that Stella Keefe was getting weaker, maybe bleeding into the thigh at the fracture. "She's 80 and has lived a full life," she said to Gill, knowing little of the depth of Stella's life, "but I think we should try to get her out."

Etien hesitated, then agreed, and after a few minutes, they took off with Stella on a stretcher, IV strapped and swinging, and Gill sitting beside her on the floor.

"I'd rather you sat up here, with a belt," Etien had said to her, pointing to the co-pilot's seat. "This is going to be bumpy."

"I'll be fine here. I'll hold on. She shouldn't be alone." The Demerol had eased Stella's pain, but she was awake enough to be aware of the hand holding hers and of the wind-pushed bouncing of the helicopter. She was also feeling increasingly calm, relieved, on the edge of being happy.

"Have you got a lot of pain?" Gill asked her, speaking very close to Stella's ear so as not to have to shout past the engine noise. Gill was ready to give more Demerol if she had to but wanted to avoid it, because she could feel the thin fast pulse and the dropping blood pressure and see the facial pallor, even with the IV going full-out.

"No, I'm fine," Stella said. "Have we crossed the Straits?"

"We've only just left, Mrs. Keefe. It'll be a while yet."

They had started south but had been slower getting away than Etien wanted, so the approaching storm had now pushed in ahead of them, cutting off the coastal route south, leaving only the chance to try to go around the edge of it by flying inland and then going either south or north, making a semi-circle. Etien saw the storm whipping in off the ocean, and the stands of trees, and the expanse of snow with animal tracks scattered at random angles. The whole thing seemed to him to be fully alive, with a force and a meaning that might not include them. He was worried about the old woman and the increasing possibility of having to put the helicopter down in the middle of the woods, and yet he felt the glee rising in him, just to be alive and riding a wind, wherever it was going. He grabbed the co-pilot's headphones and passed them back to Gill.

"We're riding a bad wind, and the weather's closing in on us, and I don't know how long I can keep going. But by sweet thundering God, isn't it beautiful up here?"

Gill looked at the back of Etien's head for some seconds before pressing the microphone he had handed her. "Just get this woman somewhere fast; that's all we're here for." She took the headphones off.

Etien flew on for about 40 more minutes, looking for a way around the storm or even back to the Nursing Station, or to another one further south on the coast. He was flying VFR, supposed to keep the ground in sight under "visual flight rules," and he didn't dare go against the book and go up over the storm, because Goose Bay Radio said they were down-in-snow, too, and so was the southern hospital. He'd made a mistake in leaving the Station, and he knew it.

The wind was gusting much higher, and the snow was getting thicker. I'm going to have to put it down, Etien thought, and he leaned back and touched Gill's arm, speaking into her ear. "I've got to land and can't get her to the hospital. I'm sorry." Gill nodded and motioned with her hand, a sign that was meant to indicate resigned acceptance, but he wasn't sure what she was saying.

Etien knew of a fishing camp, a place open only in summer for tourists, about ten miles inland up a long narrow river. He radioed Goose tower and then the hospital, telling them that they were setting down and that they were OK but that Stella Keefe was not doing well.

"Are we near the Straits yet?" Stella asked Gill, who told her no, she hoped they weren't. The two were starting to understand each other, both working against fear but doing it from opposing angles and needs.

Etien saw the camp just as he was getting ready to give up and put the machine on a pond, any pond. He waited for a lull and got it landed, shut down the engine, put his survival sleeping bag over Stella, and ran to the cabins with the hatchet from the helicopter. He smashed the lock off the smallest cabin, finding it to have two beds, blankets in a pile on one of them, and a wood stove and wood-box half full of dry wood. There were even a few tins of food in the cupboard, frozen but intact. By now the wind was in full gale, and when Etien got the fire going in the stove and ran back to the machine, he could see the fear on Gill's face.

"What are we going to do?" she said, close to panic.

"We'll be OK. That place is going to be warm in a few minutes. Let's move her over there and make it a Nursing Station. Come on, come on," he said, firmly moving her out into the wind.

They got Stella to the cabin, stumbling and almost falling with the stretcher. While Etien went out to get more wood before dark and more food from his helicopter survival gear, Gill restarted the blocked IV and tried to make Stella comfortable.

"Where are we now? Are we lost?" Stella asked once, coming up out of semiconsciousness.

"Yes, we're lost, safe in this cabin, waiting for the weather to clear, then we'll get you to hospital," Gill said, and Etien heard them as he tried to get the cabin warmer, fiddling with the damper on the stove, and heating a can of soup.

"That's good, dear. I've always been afraid of the Straits. It's good that you're here."

Gill tried to get Stella Keefe's rising pulse and blood pressure stabilized by opening up the IV, raising the bottom of the bed, and using the small amount of injectable medication she had in her emergency bag.

"I'm not going to be able to do it," she said to Etien, as she waved a "no" to the soup he handed her.

"Eat this, please. All you can do is what you can do. We could be here for days. Don't think you're stronger than the weather, because you're not and I'm not, and if she's not, there may be nothing you can do about it."

Gill took the soup and ate it. She then went to the stove and got some more, going back to Stella on the bunk bed, speaking over and over in her ear, telling her to wake up. After a while Stella said sharply "What do you want?" thinking it was the town Council chairman at her ear. Gill fed her some soup, slowly, and then talked to her, their faces close.

"Mrs. Keefe, your leg is broken, badly, and there's bleeding in there. We had to come in here because of the storm, and I can't do anything else. Do you understand me?"

"Yes, I do. You're the answer to my problem, and I want to thank you."

Gill shook her head, feeling more alone than she had in a long time, and said, "No, Stella, I can't do enough."

"Listen to me. I've always been afraid of this, because there'd be no one to wipe the mess off my face and make sure my mouth is closed and just keep the chairman away. But you're here and you've got gentle hands, and that's all I need. This is what I want, the most of anything."

Gill turned to Etien, who had come up behind her to

listen, and said, "She's not making any sense." He didn't answer, just went out to get more wood and to look for food in the other cabins, anything to be doing something.

Overnight the wind became even stronger, and with the cabin having no insulation and the wind pushing in through every crack, even a full fire barely kept it warm. Etien offered to sit with Stella while Gill got some sleep, but she refused. The wind and storm became more and more of a rage, to the point that Etien almost got lost just going to check the tie-down ropes on the helicopter. When he came in, there was a difference in the room and he went to the bed right away.

"She's dead," said Gill, not looking at him, "just a few minutes ago. She didn't make a sound, just stopped breathing. Her heart is still doing occasional beats, but she's gone." Stella lay on her back, with the IV out now, and twice a long sighing sound came from her. Etien guided Gill over to the other bed, helped her lie down and covered her with several blankets. She lay on her side, facing the cabin wall.

After a while, Gill got up and went over to Stella Keefe and started to get ready to "do up the body," to prepare it for the death pose.

"I want to help," Etien said.

"No."

"Listen, I need to help, for me if not for you, and for her too. Just because you're the nurse and I'm the taxi driver doesn't mean that old woman didn't touch me. Her death is just the way she wanted, so don't make things bad because we couldn't give her more time."

They washed Stella carefully, closed her eyes and mouth, packed the rectum, and dressed her as gently as possible, both of them thinking without talking that this body had worked and loved and had babies, and had even known the full extent of its apparent permanence.

Gill led Etien through all of this with calm ritual but then didn't know what to do when they finished.

"Can we put her in the helicopter?" she asked.

Etien said, "It's blowing too hard. We could get lost going even that far in the dark. She can stay here with us tonight." They covered her with a blanket, hesitating before placing it over her face.

Gill lay down on the other bed, and Etien covered her with blankets, touching her shoulder for a few seconds. He sat up all night and kept the fire going in the small stove, sitting on the edge of the bed by Gill whenever she woke up. Once he went out to the helicopter to try to reach people by radio but failed. The storm was holding.

Near morning, Gill turned over to face him and made room under the blankets. Etien lay down, putting his arms around her, and she pushed her head down close to his chest and went to sleep.

When they woke up, it was light and the cabin was freezing, with the wind shaking the walls and roof. Etien got the fire going and put soup and canned beans on the stove. He brought in some snow and melted it in basins and pots and a kettle on top of the stove. They washed their faces without talking and then went out looking for an outhouse. The wind owned them, choking back breath, pushing at them and then changing directions so they'd almost fall, making it very easy to get lost. It was colder than yesterday and this storm could kill them quickly if they weren't careful.

After they found and used the outhouse, they fought their way through the wind back to the cabin, put Stella on the stretcher and carried her to the helicopter. It took them over fifteen minutes to go the few hundred feet to the clearing and back, and there were several very bad moments when Etien was sure he'd lost the path back to the cabin. When they finally got in they ate in silence, watching the wind blast snow against the windows and feeling the walls shake. Looking out through a cleared spot they had rubbed on the fogged and icing window, all they could see was a fierce white wall, changing its folding shape like a wind-driven blanket on a clothesline.

"Are we safe here?" Gill asked.

"Yes. I've got lots of wood, and the other cabins had enough cans and bits of food to last us about a week."

"A *week*! How long can this go on? I don't know how long I can stand it."

"You don't have a lot of choices. Would it help to talk, instead of these long silences?"

"It usually doesn't help, not at all. I should thank you for holding me last night. That was one of the worst nights of my life."

"I needed to be held too, you know. The old woman died because I made a mistake; we didn't get her to the hospital, and we didn't stay at the Station. I blew it."

Gill looked startled, brought sharply into awareness. "Her name is, was, Stella Keefe, not 'old woman,' and she probably would have died at the Station. We'd no one to do the surgery, and no blood, and I have more medication in that bag than the Station had. And you heard what she said, it's what she wanted. I don't understand that."

"There's probably a lot of things about her life we haven't got the faintest clue about. Same for everybody." They didn't talk for a while, with Etien making them some tea, Labrador style, strong with sugar and Carnation milk. He sat down at the table with Gill and looked at her.

"Why were you so sharp when we were in the air and a couple of times since? Is that just you, or is something else going on?"

"We don't want to talk about this now, not now. Just leave it alone."

"Yes, *we* do; now's the only time there is. What is going on?"

"I've heard about you, from the Station nurses, that you sleep with anyone and everyone all along the coast and don't care who you hurt or why. I wanted to be cold with you, still do. I think your way of dealing with people is wrong. I don't want to like you, and if all this hadn't happened, I wouldn't give you the time of day."

"You're pretty sure you've got my number, my life cased, without knowing me at all. You have no idea of what my life is or who I care for. I'm curious—did all these people who warned you about me say I was a mean person, uncaring, a liar, someone who used people for sex?"

"No, nobody said those things. But I've met a couple of people who you've hurt quite badly. Maybe you don't even know it. They think they *love* you, for God's sake, and you just get in your helicopter and fly away. Don't you have any notion of how vulnerable and scared and lonely a lot of people are?"

"Yes, I do. I see those things, and maybe they hold on to me because they see that I'm just as scared and lonely as they are."

"You? I don't think so."

"Why not? What do you know about it, or me? You might benefit from shaking your box of biases occasionally. A couple of examples—why do you assume that I'm the one hurting people and not the one getting hurt or used? And why do you assume that sex is at the bottom of everything and not other things like affection and loneliness and fear? You and I slept together last night, and don't you think there won't be talk about *that* up and down the coast? It seemed to me it was pretty equal, and it certainly wasn't about sex."

Etien got up and put on his parka and went out into the wind, fighting his way to the helicopter, checked the ropes, and then climbed in. He touched Stella where he knew her shoulder would be, under the blanket, and turned on the engine. He spent the next half hour trying to reach either the airport or the base hospital, finally getting through instead to the nearest Nursing Station. He told them that Stella Keefe had died and asked this to be relayed to the family and nurse, and to the airline and the hospital, and he told them that he and Gill were safe, sitting and waiting out the storm in a tourist cabin.

There was a long pause from the Station when he gave this information, finally getting it understood through the static, then the person receiving the call said, "Roger HAB, I check your message. I'm sorry. Are you sure you and the nurse are OK? We could maybe try to get to you by skidoo." He told her that they were fine, and they arranged a time to call, every six hours on this frequency. He signed off and shut down the engine.

On his way back to the cabin, Etien fell several times in drifts he couldn't see until he was in them. As he came into the cabin, Gill stood up and said, " I thought you were flying away when I heard the engine."

"We're in this together. When I go, you go. OK?"

"Yes."

"I was able to get through to Mary's Harbour. They know what's happening. Everybody will be notified, including Stella Keefe's family."

He made some more tea. Gill said, "I've been sitting here thinking about what you said. But don't you realize that you're not making a commitment to anyone and that people want that from you? I happen to know of a couple who do at least. They feel they were misled."

"I didn't mean to. There's so much of this that I just don't get. Like how trying to be caring can be wrong, and why people don't worry more about the quality of the touch, and the origin of it, instead of the location. I also simply do not understand why it is assumed, a given, a goddamn immutable *law*, that if two people are close then the links with other people are false or diminished. What cultural need is met by this exclusivity clause in the affection contract?"

"Not in the affection contract, just in the sexual one—the *love* one."

"But *why*? The degree of intimacy we had last night, and now for that matter, is more than with a lot of sexual encounters in my past. That's part of the point, of what I'm trying to do with my life, to make the connections real, to make them mean something."

"That's what's so sad. You're working against your own aim. You won't have many friends by the time you're fifty, at least not women."

"And you, Gill, with your cool distance and judgements? Will you?"

"Not very many, but more than you, I think. I do want to find *one* for sure, man or woman, I don't care, and then not betray that person."

"If you find someone who feels betrayed because you care for other people, then he or she will have betrayed *you*."

"I don't believe in what you say. It may be true for you, but it's not for me, and I don't think it is for most people.

I'll tell you one thing: you don't understand women. And I don't think you understand yourself."

They stopped talking and just fed the fire, and heard the wind on the cabin walls. Gill went to sleep, and Etien sat at the table, thinking about what she'd said and what others had said. He was trying to remember the lines to an old Randy Newman song, something about "maybe I'm doing it wrong," without "it" ever being specified. Then he remembered a woman who had once shared his room and who would sometimes wake in the middle of the night shouting her mother's name and crying. She was smart and strong and hated to be seen naked. He still had a bracelet of hers and a pair of green socks. Gill was watching him from the bed and saw the tears on his face. She got up and put her hand on his, then brushed away the wetness, carefully.

They barely spoke for the rest of the day. Etien noticed that Gill's lips were dry and cracked, and he dug out a tube of vaseline from a pocket, hesitated, and then said, "May I?" She nodded, and he gently coated her lips, using his fingers.

In the evening, they talked at the table, sitting close, speaking quietly, and often looking directly at each other's faces. They told of parents who had died, and of important promises, central places of home, and even of the worst fears. They were not surprised at how many similarities they found, frequently just nodding in agreement or recognition at a shared fact or opinion.

In the morning the wind was easing. They had sat up all night and were exhausted, so they slept for a few hours, on separate beds, then straightened up the cabin, leaving a thank-you note and money for food and locks. The wind was still blowing, but the storm was over.

"Let's go, Gill."

"I almost hate to leave. We were making progress, don't you think?"

"We'll see. I hope so."

They flew toward the base hospital, staying low because of the heavy overcast, following the shoreline to the nearest village, where Etien gassed up the machine. Then they went over the Straits, with Gill keeping her hand on Stella Keefe all the way across. When they landed beside the hospital, people were there right away, anxious, concerned, sympathetic.

Etien helped them carry the stretcher out of the helicopter, with Gill watching. One of the radio operators told Gill that the hospital plane would be taking her back that afternoon and that she'd better go talk to the head nurse.

As she turned away, Gill saw Etien sitting at the controls of the helicopter, watching her. She waved, and he nodded and motioned with his hand, but she didn't know what he meant; she didn't recognize the sign of resigned acceptance. The helicopter lifted off, flying south.

As she walked toward the hospital, Gill felt the lip-vaseline tube in her pocket and without hesitating she threw it out into the snow.

Thick with Rabbits

The ship from Labrador, the *Sir Robert Bond*, came into St. John's through the narrow harbour entrance. The wind that had been so strong minutes before, face on, abruptly just stopped, blocked by the hills. Etien Rich still shivered but nevertheless felt warmer as he passed the houses on the left, and the lighthouse, and then he turned to look at the Battery. He always felt a familiarity with the Battery houses, even though he hadn't earned it. A magazine article had talked of the difficulties for the residents in obtaining water and getting rid of sewage, with the rock cliffs steep and with ledges to the water edge. The magazine had been on an empty chair in the TV lounge of the Bond, which had doubled as a bedroom for Etien and about ten other people on the three-day trip from Goose Bay. He leaned on the starboard rail, looking carefully at the houses, trying to weigh their stability and their defiance. The harbour was calm, and the ship moved slowly in, not going toward the dock at Water Street as Etien had expected but instead easing into another straight ahead from the Narrows, near the Battery. The whistle blew, and he jumped even though he had braced for it.

Etien watched the crew do their work with ropes, and the engines sidled the ship into the dock with a slam and grinding of timber. Soon the people were leaving by the roped-in walkway, and he continued to lean on the rail of the upper deck and watch—the ones he had avoided and the ones who had avoided him, the majority of others who didn't care one way or the other, and the two or three who had talked and listened. One man stopped and looked up at the bow where Etien was leaning and motioned as if to say, "Are you coming or not?" Etien shook his head and waved good-bye. The man took off his old grey felt hat with a mock grandiose sweeping gesture, bowed and then left with his two huge foolish dogs on a leash.

Etien walked up Water Street. The backpack was too heavy, and he ritualistically cursed his vanity at bringing extra pants and shirts. The boots were good-for-it though. I love the boots, he thought, and then smiled grimly at his use of the word "love," remembering the recent nasty debates about its use, on the boat and off. A boy walked by without looking at him. The pack dug at Etien's shoulders, and even in the cold and wind he was sweating, but he was also feeling happier and stronger with every step. The boy, aged about 12, had turned and looked at Etien after they passed. He saw a man in his thirties, with long black hair, wearing a short thick light-brown jacket and jeans and carrying a backpack, a blue knitted toque on his head, and since he was not wearing gloves, his hands were red from the cold. He was leaning into the pack and looking around as if trying to find the source of a pleasant sound. I'd like to have a backpack like that, the boy thought.

Etien walked until he found a cheap hotel near the waterfront. Walking into the lobby, he almost hit a woman with the pack as he swung out of it. "Sorry," he said. She didn't answer. The lobby easily held two hard-backed chairs, both empty, a cigarette machine, and an out-of-order pop machine. There was linoleum on the floor and the desk clerk was safely caged behind steel mesh. Welcome home, Etien thought, feeling again the familiar mix of loneliness and necessary privacy.

"How much for a single room?," he asked.

"$40 a night and a $5 deposit for your key; get it back when you go," said the desk clerk, without looking up from his newspaper.

"Anything cheaper?"

"No."

"OK."

"How many nights?"

"Two, I think."

"I need to know for sure."

"One."

He signed the card and gave the $45. He had paused at the address portion of the card, before filling in "Grand Lake, Labrador."

"What kind of name is Etien?," the clerk asked, having noticed the pause. He was about 25, tall and bony, with large random hands and arms and feet, and a pale face that was neither hostile nor friendly. I could have been a desk clerk, Etien thought, taking a long look at the man through the steel mesh.

"It's an Acadian name, maybe French to you. Why?"

"Just wondered; I collect names. Room 18, up the stairs."

Etien picked up the pack again and went up the stairs, very narrow, then up more stairs. The low-numbered rooms were at the top. Symbolism is truly a wonderful thing, he thought.

The room had a bed, chair, sink, a lamp on a small desk, a tiny window facing a nearby brick wall, and it was warm. He took off his boots, which weren't even hiking boots guaranteed to inspire affection but just old Kodiak work boots which fit his feet perfectly, then his jeans and high-necked, thick, blue sweater, throwing it all in a pile on his cowhide jacket. He felt free and lonely, but mostly his back hurt.

Etien had washed and was lying on the bed, easing into a doze, when the door opened. He wasn't asleep enough to be confused but just sat up and said, "What?" The woman, in a uniform and with towels in her hand, laughed at him and asked if he wanted any towels. He took two and noticed as the door closed that the inside lock was busted. He got into bed, rolled onto his right side, and went to sleep.

The next morning he got up early and just started out without bothering to eat. He walked the streets of St. John's again, from the harbour past the convent, remembering the Sisters' cafeteria and the marble bust with the illusion of a veil, past homes and hills to the Avalon Mall and on to the University, where he spent $2.50 on tea and toast. He then went up to Confederation Building, standing and watching the flow of the city from the steps, and chatting about ice-pans and hubris with Grenfell's statue before starting back to the harbour. Always back to the harbour, inspecting the fishing boats and freighters that were tied up, walking slowly back and forth along the wharf. Etien found the Employment and Immigration office and, after standing there for two hours, had lunch in the Bowring's cafeteria. He then worked his way back to the hotel, feeling glad for the heavy dull ache of tiredness in his legs, and told the clerk that he wanted to stay one more night.

"Good," the clerk said, "Real good. Especially since you've missed the check-out time by six hours."

Etien's money was running out, and it was September with very little work available in St. John's or anywhere else on the island. It also seemed that he had very little to offer for a price. "What skills have you got?" the Employment and Immigration people had asked, both in Goose and in St. John's. "None at the moment," Etien had said, and now thought it was a pity he couldn't market his walking skills—guided tour to the touch and pulse of St. John's, or Black Tickle, Dead Islands, Triangle, Rigolet, Nain, Davis Inlet, Fox Harbour, Norman Bay, North West River, Port Hope Simpson; wherever they wanted.

No such luck, but it was their loss. The Employment and Immigration person and he had finally reached an understanding that he was an ex-bush pilot, now un-licensed because of some official awkwardness with Labrador Airways. There was no work available, he was told.

The next morning, at 8 o'clock, he was at the CN bus and train station, waiting for the Road Cruiser to Port Aux Basques. Are you on the bus or off the bus, he thought, and wasn't amused. A recorded voice announced the departure, and he joined people going toward Bus #2.

He put the pack down near the driver, who was load-ing baggage, and moved quickly into the bus, hoping for the right front seat. The seat was empty. Other people came in and then the driver, a tall large man with sharp eyes, dark hair straight back from his forehead, and a deep voice, said, "Whoever owns that knapsack by the bus had better load it or it gets left here." Etien quickly got up and out of the bus, red-faced and silently cursing, and put the pack in the baggage compartment, then got back into his seat. The driver came down the aisle, punching tickets.

"Sorry about the pack. I didn't realize I was supposed to hand it to you." Truly humiliated, and yet a part of him watching the whole scene, separate.

"Everyone else seemed to know," said the driver, full of indignant righteousness but softening when he saw no fight in Etien. "That's OK, anyway. Where you going to?"

"Port Aux Basques, then Nova Scotia."

"You belong to there?" the driver asked.

"No; sometimes."

"Good day for a long drive."

"Yeah. That's what I thought."

Best seat in the bus and what the hell if I had to earn it, Etien thought. Mile after mile in sun and twisting pot-holed highway. Good to be moving again, he thought. There were kids holding dead rabbits upside down by the feet, by the side of the road, dozens of them for sale at $7 a pair.

"Rabbits are thick," said the driver over his shoulder.

Etien fixed on the road, as it wound and unwound. The bus stopped in Gander for lunch and Cornerbrook for supper. They drove through the Humber Valley at sun-down, with the trees matching the sun red for red. The bus pulled into Port Aux Basques at 11:00 pm, near the dock. Etien walked onto the ferry, paying $2 extra for a reclining seat—a "Day-Nighter." He then wandered the decks of the ferry, getting a feel of it. He walked through the TV lounge, where *The National* was on in colour, with Peter Mansbridge a light shade of green. There were people on deck in pairs, the cafeteria was closed, and tables sat round and bolted to the deck, small enough for one or two people. He felt that he belonged to the place.

The bus driver had suddenly said to him early that morning, near the turnoff to Fortune, "Where *do* you belong to?" and Etien had replied, "Grand Lake, the Labrador one," easing gratefully into the memory of the cabin and walks on the miles of shore. The driver hadn't bothered with him anymore. I belong *here*, he thought, on the boat, and asked a crew member for a blanket and pillow, sleeping in the chair for about three hours.

Etien walked off the boat at North Sydney, at 6:00 am, in the dark.

Tide Flats

Etien Rich was helping Charlie Williams prepare for the first day of the fall apple harvest, putting the empty boxes and ladders in the orchards, always managing to take longer in the one stand of trees that faced Blomidon. He sometimes watched the sun colour the slope of that bluff, while on other days clouds and mist would move over and around it. The angle of its wooded red-earth jutting into the Bay of Fundy gradually asserted itself on his line of view, as he became aware that this hill might be more than a hill. Etien had asked Charlie many questions about growing apples but still knew absolutely nothing about the whole business. He did know about the weight of the apples pulling down the branches, the cool early morning fog drifting over the soaked grass, and the long reach of the red-mud tide flats of the Minas Basin, the widest and most shallow inlet of the Bay of Fundy.

Etien had been in the shed for two weeks, alone, sleeping in a double bed near the window at the far end of the narrow sloped-ceilinged rough-walled attic, taking time to get used to the temperament of the wood-burning box heater. At first he had to pile his jacket and clothes on the bed to keep warm at night, after the fire went out, but Emily Williams had noticed the clothes on the bed one morning when she came to wake him and had brought over two large quilts that evening. The quilts were skillfully made, intricate, balanced, bright and deep in colour, and warm at night. Etien was careful with them.

It soon became obvious that the Williamses were not used to having hired help, or were used to treating their help as family. Becoming a part of the household, of the schedule and interactions, seemed to happen too quickly. It should be awkward, Etien thought. The meals and work included him and had a rhythm he had gone without for such a long time that he was initially uncomfortable when it fit him.

George, the 10-year-old son, was desperate for someone to play catch with him and to explore the 50 acres of woodland that the Williamses owned about a mile away. Etien noticed George's ability to enjoy his time and found himself relearning the same skill. He found himself becoming familiar again with the feel of baseball seams, the routes and tangled corners of brooks, and the eerie flick of bats at dusk. Etien saw that Charlie viewed George's increasing attachment to him with some relief but also with some pain. They didn't talk about this.

Iris, Charlie and Emily's 23-year-old daughter, had seemed unfriendly at first. As Etien and the family relaxed with each other, he saw her as simply being generally unhappy, and they rarely spoke to each other. George looked more like his mother than Iris did, with his light brown hair and clear bright blue eyes, short stature and fullness of arms and legs, and although George was always bounding around while Emily was quiet and controlled, they shared an aura of optimism and contentment. Iris looked more like her father, taller and lean, with dark brown hair left long and straight on her back, grey eyes and a brooding mouth that could turn on you. A smile had to be wrenched from Charlie and Iris, a quick flash that escaped them.

Soon after hiring on at the Williamses', Etien went with Charlie into Canning, the nearest community with a hardware store. Etien left Charlie at the store and found other places where he could use his remaining money to buy a heavy, dark-green cotton shirt; a pair of work gloves; soap and toothpaste; a round, red, plastic wash basin; a small mirror in a white wood frame; the paperback edition of *World of Wonders*; and six colours of fine-point, felt-tip pens.

When they got home, Etien went to the attic and set up a washstand and then put his new Davies Penguin and some old books on the window ledge by his bed. The Etien Rich Blomidon Memorial Library, he thought, admiring the washstand, bed with quilt, and window over the bed, more pleased with himself than he had been in a long time.

Emily usually visited the shed in the mornings to wake Etien, coming up the stairs at about 6 o'clock, with the window still grey dark and the attic cold. Sometimes she would start the fire for him, sometimes not. Occasionally Charlie had the waking duty, and he would just shout up from the bottom of the stairs. "Good sleeper," he said to Etien at breakfast, with his quick darting grin. The morning after Etien bought the washbasin, he was up early, having wakened with a start without knowing why, and was sponge-bathing at the washstand when Emily came up the stairs. He didn't cover himself or warn her away, feeling that would be foolish and harmful to them both. She was surprised to see him naked, but he quickly said, "It's okay Emily; I'm up, just having a quick bath. I'll be over in a few minutes."

"You can use the tub in the house, you know," she said, standing at the top of the stairs looking at him, without expression in her face or voice.

"I don't feel that easy yet in your house, maybe in a while. And I enjoy washing like this, with a fire in the heater. Feels like home."

She looked away and went down the steps, not saying anything. After breakfast she gave him four thick towels and faceclothes, saying, "You need to put on some weight; start eating some more, why don't you." Iris heard this as she cleared the table and looked up, puzzled, but didn't stop moving. After this Emily and Charlie didn't wake him in the mornings, and Etien began to wake at about 5:30 without being called.

The harvest started, and the other pickers moved into the attic. John Shand and a man they called "Dummy," a deaf-mute, came from the Shands' place about five miles down the road toward Canning. John was about 25, a big dark-haired solemn man, who walked as if he wasn't comfortable in his body but seemed sure of himself in the way he used his eyes and hands. Etien held out his hand to the second man, who was bone thin and had no top teeth, with a resultant overwhelming smile. Hard to know how old he is, Etien thought, probably in his forties.

"What's his real name?" he asked John Shand.

"Paul, I think, but everybody calls him Dummy. No harm meant by it, just his name. He can lip read some and knows Dummy means him. If you call him Paul, he won't know what you're saying. He's the best picker that Charlie's got."

John stayed in the house and talked with Iris after supper, and while it was obvious they had known each other for many years and quickly understood the other's feelings, and even though Iris had far more to say at supper than usual, there didn't appear to be any depth of either affection or hostility between the two, just a neutral intimacy.

Etien, George and Paul went to the shed attic and played Crazy Eights. Etien had said "Paul" and pointed to Paul, then "Etien" and pointed to himself. Paul shook his head and made an "M" motion with his mouth. When Etien shook his head and repeated the Paul-point routine, Paul just shrugged, rolled his eyes and laughed.

The next day Etien and Charlie were in one corner of the orchard alone, with Charlie showing the basics of apple picking, such as the method of propping the ladder with its pointed end against the tree limbs. "You have to wedge it in at a fork," Charlie said, "so you won't fall. You'd bruise all the apples in your sack if you fell." He demonstrated how to pick with both hands, using the waist-level shallow sack that he had given to Etien, and then how to empty the sack into the boxes placed along the row of trees without bruising every apple.

"John and Iris good friends?" Etien asked, as they stopped and looked back along the orchard path. Iris was setting up to pick and had selected a tree near John.

"They've known each other all their lives, but it comes and goes. They were real close a couple of years ago. Have gone to school together, and everything else, since they were kids." Charlie paused, and Etien waited. "John wanted to get married, but she said no. I was glad she did. John's alright, but he's got no life in him. Maybe I was wrong, though, because all she does now is sit around." Another pause. "She talk to you?"

189

"No," said Etien.

After supper that night, Etien found that his inclination to hold on to the tree with one hand while he was up the ladder, gently and slowly depositing every apple into the sack, had been noted by Iris and Charlie. Paul had picked five times Etien's output.

"It's a damn good thing you chose daily pay. You'd starve to death otherwise," said Charlie, with mock disgust. Paul watched them laughing, not understanding, smiling anyway. Charlie pointed to Paul and made very rapid apple picking motions with both hands, then to Etien and did an extremely slow one-handed picking pantomime, complete with frightened glances toward the floor. Paul roared a laugh, a strange sound that startled all of them, and then repeated the entire scene, delighted to be recognized in his dominance.

George was coming out to the shed attic most evenings now, in spite of school, as his parents knew this wouldn't last and let it be. In the orchard the next day Charlie said to Etien, "George asked me if he could move out to the shed while the picking's going on. Is he bothering you?"

"No, it's good to have him around," Etien said. "He can have the extra bed. We all go to sleep pretty early, around 10. That okay?"

"Sure, that's fine. Looks as if Davis isn't coming this year, so the bed's empty. First time in five years he hasn't come from New Brunswick. Strange man, but it's hard to get anyone else to come work, and he's fine anyway."

When George showed up in the orchard at 4:30, after school, Charlie told him he could move into the attic. They all went home an hour later, walking. In the yard was a 1949 Pontiac, dark blue, covered with several colours of hand-lettered place-names. "It's Davis," said George, unhappy because this meant he had lost his place in the attic. The car was in good shape, clean with no rust, and the rugs on the floor and the heavy rope handrail on the back of the front seat looked like new. The place-names had been carefully printed, hundreds of them with no obvious pattern of geography or sound—Kentville, Toronto, Calgary, North Rustico, Kenora, Sackville, Norway House, Banff, Goose Bay, Peace River, Yellowknife, Winnipeg, and on and on. Davis was in the house, at the table, a short thick man of about 55, with thin hair, a tight mouth, and eyes that didn't bother with you. He nodded to Etien when Charlie introduced them. Not a man to chat about the political situation in New Brunswick, Etien thought, and they ate quietly.

After supper Davis and Paul went out to the shed, with the rest staying in the kitchen. Etien and Iris dried the dishes. Emily was washing, while Charlie, George and John sat at the table. Charlie was glancing at George, who sat with his face glum.

"George, looks like you'll have to sleep with me in the double bed. Think you can stand that?" asked Etien, pleased to see the looks given him by Emily and Charlie.

Iris kept on wiping dishes, as George ran out of the kitchen to get his things. "That's nice, Etien," she said, glancing his way.

The next week went cleanly, with Etien coming back to the attic every evening tired and full of the feel of apples and leaves and ladders, the sight of clouds and grass, the hum of the day. John and Iris spent much time walking and talking, but they had the look of always circling back to the same place.

George had brought a table-hockey game out to the

shed, an old one that used a marble and had players that twirled but didn't move back and forth. He, Paul and Etien played every night. Etien had played the game before, years ago and very often. Paul, with his quick reflexes and ability to concentrate so completely on one thing, soon became very good at it as well. George practiced at the game, setting up angles, planning deflections. Davis occasionally watched them play but spent most of his time writing in a blue-covered writing pad every evening. "He's okay. Don't worry about him," Charlie had said, when Etien asked about Davis.

They didn't pick on Sunday, and the family, except Iris, went to Canning to see Charlie's brother and family. John and Paul had gone back to Shands' on Saturday evening, and Davis stayed in the shed attic all day. It was a hot sunny day in early October, a return of summer with autumn temporarily put on hold. There would be cold rain in two weeks and soon after that an early snow, but not on this day.

Etien took two apples from a tree and walked to the cliff, finding a ravine to get down to the beach. It was low tide. He took off his boots and socks, leaving them on the beach, then went far out on the mud flats, almost a mile, walking along the water's edge toward the cottages at Medford. Minas Basin has huge tides as the ocean funnels in through the narrow Bay of Fundy, and these swings in water level combine with the shallow tidal shelf to give over a mile of "beach" at low tide, only much of the beach is not sand but thick red mud.

There were no people out on the flats. Calendar slaves, Etien thought, and as he was so far out from the houses on the bank, he took off and carried all his clothes, walking along the water's cold foamy edge, feeling the sun warm him. The last time for about eight months, he thought. There hadn't been much walking lately, and his thighs were soon aching, surprising him because his legs had been hard and strong a month before. There were many seagulls floating in the water and perched on rocks, with others wading and circling in the air. After walking for about an hour, he turned and went back, putting on his clothes while far out from the cliff. His boots were still there, side by side at the base of the red-mud bank.

Etien went into the house when he got back, but the family still wasn't home. He hesitated and then opened the fridge and cupboards, making sandwiches, debating whether to take a beer. He heard Iris call from upstairs, "John, come on up," and then the sound of tub water running.

Etien went to the bottom of the stairs and said, "Iris, it's Etien. I'm just making a sandwich. Do you want anything?"

There was a pause before Iris said, "No, thanks. I thought I heard John come in; sorry."

Etien went back to the kitchen and finished the sandwiches, not taking a beer. He was washing his dishes when he heard Iris say "Etien" from upstairs, not loudly. He had been wondering if she would, waiting, expecting it but startled nevertheless. When he went up to the bathroom, Iris was standing dripping on the bath mat beside the tub, just watching him as he came near. Etien reached behind her and took down a thick yellow towel, then dried her, carefully, beginning with her face. He moved the towel gently over her back, shoulders and arms, then her chest and abdomen, then slowly dried her legs and feet. Iris stood with one hand on the wall, relaxed and with her eyes closed. Etien traced her eyes and mouth with his fingertips, feeling close to her but also tired, at the beginning of a place he'd been before, a place he knew to be more risky than being alone.

Iris put her arms around him and rested her face on his chest. "Hello," she said, quietly.

After a minute, Etien asked "What do you want, Iris?" She started to speak then stopped, seeming to wait for her own answer. "I don't know. I wish I did."

"When are your folks coming home?"

"Any minute now, and John's coming over for supper; he called. Do you see?"

Etien stepped back, slowly, keeping one hand on her shoulder while handing her the towel. She held it, looking at him, and said, "Can I dry you like that, in the attic, when the apples are done?"

Etien nodded, then left, going back to the shed, taking a beer from the fridge on the way. He heard the sound of two cars coming in about fifteen minutes later, as he lay on his bed.

The next few days moved according to the ritual of the apple harvest, with many other things left unresolved and unsaid, but it was difficult to tell whether they were ignored or accepted. John and Iris walked and talked less, seeming to have reached a dead end. A recurrent one, Etien guessed, not wanting to know what it was, but Charlie had to talk about it, as he was feeling old and vulnerable watching them.

"She had a baby two years ago, John's I suppose, and put it up for adoption. That hurt Emily about as much as anything I ever saw, but Iris said it was going to be done her way or she'd leave. She won't talk about it, but she's been different since. She wouldn't marry John, before or then or now. I don't know what drives the girl."

"It's not John," Etien allowed himself to say.

"No, it's not John," Charlie said, looking up quickly.

Wednesday night was set for the table-hockey playoffs, with George, Etien and Paul being in "the finals," because they were the only entries. Etien had made a trophy by gluing a tin can to a piece of wood, the can polished to shine like silver once the tomato juice label was off. Blomidon Cup was written on it in felt pen. George and Paul had become very good at the game, but Etien was still the usual winner. John, Charlie and Davis were all watching the finals, with Emily and Iris coming into the attic for a few minutes to satisfy George, then leaving. Iris brushed her hand against Etien's arm as she left, not taking particular care to hide the gesture.

The players drew for bye in the first round, with George winning. Etien and Paul faced off, best four of seven, with five goals winning a game. Paul was very fast with his hands, reacting instantly to any shift of Etien's players. Etien saw that everyone except George was hoping for Paul to win and trying not to show it, except for Davis, who openly clapped Paul on the back with each of his goals. Etien liked him for this, regretting not having made any effort to talk to the man, to look under his surly face, at what made him write place-names on an old, well-cared-for car, and make long notes in thick pads.

Paul and Etien were tied three games each, then four goals each in the last game. A promoter's dream, thought Etien, Hockey Night in Blomidon. He faked a shot with his left winger, something he had done rarely, being content to play it straight and saving Paul's tendency to overreact to fakes as insurance. The faked shot brought Paul's goalie over, allowing Etien's centre to deflect in a pass. Paul's face jumped open, hurt, soundless, then closed and just gave out his usual protective smile. Etien was glad and sorry, feeling the winner's pity and anger. The same old thing, he thought. John, Charlie and Davis didn't say anything, but George said "good game" to both, to Paul with a thumbs-up gesture.

Etien and George started to play, with Etien hoping he would lose but refusing to throw it. I didn't get to this elite position by diving in table hockey, he thought, looking out at the attic. George had been practicing to advantage and knew how to position his goalie to block the quick hard shots from defense that Etien liked to use. Etien was leading, though, three games to two, and four goals to two in the sixth game, when he positioned his right wing's stick in the line of his shot from defense, deflecting it in.

"You played really well, George," Etien said. "I've had a lot of practice. The next time I'm not sure there'll be anyone to handle you." But George was low and the room was quiet. Davis and Paul started a card game, and John soon went home.

Charlie put his hands on Etien's and George's shoulders and said, "Let's go have something to eat."

In the house, Iris was standing at the counter and asked Etien if he wanted tea, smiling when he said thanks, but he'd get it himself. He asked her to sit down to talk with him. George started to ask him about fixing the basketball hoop, which was slanting toward the ground.

"Maybe tomorrow," said Etien, then added, "tomorrow for sure."